TALES OF THE STARPEOPLE:

Escape on the High Seas

by
Valerie Frank and Bridget Davis

Copyright 1996
Wishstar Publishing
P.O. Box 995
Trinidad, Ca 95570
All rights reserved

ISBN: 9780983584216
Library of Congress Control Number: 2012936691

PROLOGUE
(DORENA 1633, England)

"There is no one time, or one place, that can hold the Nation of the Starpeople." the man announced loudly, and then he disappeared. No one in the crowded village had seen him move even one step from where he had been standing next to the goat pens, yet he was gone. A few muttered prayers were heard, but for the most part, no one spoke, instead just shaking their heads and slowly returning to their homes. Once safely indoors, many just sighed, and discussed the events they were planning for the `morrow, while others thought to spend the night in silent reflection. Dorena was having none of it. At twenty years of age and newly wed, she felt the curiosity of youth and asked her husband, a respectable blacksmith, what he had made of it all. "Probably should wait till the church Elders have a chance to discuss it, don't you think? It might be unholy, or unlucky, or something." This made Dorena smile, since she knew Brand, her husband, did not hold to any church doctrine. It was simply his way of saying that he had no idea how to answer her question. She did not know what had just happened in her village either, and that fact excited her like nothing she had ever experienced. Had she witnessed magic? Had Old Man Tremor been right all along? The old drunk had said it himself many times...

"They will come for me! Straight from the stars, they will come for me. Just watch!" And now they had.

"Write it down, will you Brand?" she asked her husband.

While some men taught their wives to read and write, it was considered unseemly and frivolous for a woman to spend time away from her work of tending the home. Being raised in a strict house, Dorena had grown up in the traditional way, and so had no education of her own apart from the skills her mother had taught her. Now her young husband smiled, "Don't you trust my memory?"

She hugged him tightly, knowing he was teasing her still. "Of course I do, but this..." She raised her arms to the ceiling of their modest home's thatched roof, but her gaze went beyond, to the reaches of the sky, "...this was something! Something really big! I want it to be in our records, for our grandchildren to see."

This time the young husband did not smile, but sighed. "Dorena. I told you before, my beloved. No one will believe this. Everyone thinks so. Even the Deacon agreed, he would not be reporting this. What you purpose would only serve to confuse our grandchildren. Perhaps we should follow the Elder's advice on this one. We say nothing; we record

4

nothing, until they have had a chance to meet upon it." She was about to protest, when he added, "Let us just wait until after their meeting. Then we can discuss it again, if we decide to."

A few days later, when Brand returned from the town meeting, he was quiet. She had promised herself she would not press him, and it was not until after their small dinner, and they were alone in the bed he had made for her that he whispered, "They have told us to forget what we have seen."

She could not see him well in the dying firelight, but she could tell by his voice that he was just as shocked by the statement as she was. They got little sleep that night, whispering at one time their outrage at being directed to do such a deed, and other times planning just how they would record the "event" and where. It was decided that they would write it in their family Bible, the only book they owned. They had considered impressing it upon leather, the common form to record daily records, easily pressed out and used again. But they felt leather would not stand the test of time, for many creatures might eat the stuff. But the Bible was meant to be treasured, and passed from one generation to another, so it was this they decided upon. Brand had bought it for his wife as a present when he had asked for her hand in marriage. It was the newest version, freshly translated from Latin. He knew how much his betrothed loved to be read to, from any book, and since he himself could not read Latin, this rendition

5

of the Bible served the needs of them both. It had a cover made of maple wood, nicely polished, and bored with holes along the edges, where leather had been sown while soft, and after wetted with vinegar just long the spine, was allowed to dry hard, while leaving the edges soft for opening the cover with out breaking. With the tools of his trade he had carved their names into the cover, burning the wood deep enough so that he felt they would never be rubbed off.

It had ample space for recording family information, births, deaths, etc., and it was in the pages for recording births that they decided to write the account of their experience. They chose a place about half way down knowing that , one day, the record would be somewhat hidden among the other recorded births that would occur in their new family, throughout the following generations. But not too far down that they would not be found by some future family member curious enough to look.

"Old Man Tremor told us," Brand read aloud to Dorena as he wrote on the page, slowly, as not to make mistakes."He was old when I was born, and he had always insisted that there were folks from the stars for as long as I can recall. We thought he told such tales because he was drunk, but now we know, he drank because he had such tales to tell and no one would believe him." Brand stopped, looking at Dorena for her approval, and at her smile and nod, continued on the next entry, having run out of room. "In this year of our Lord 1633, we, my wife and I, did see a ship dock to a cloud above our village square. Many people were there and also professed to see it. I do not know ships, but it had three masts and we could see dozens of hands moving upon it. Clearly we could see a stout rope, stretched before it and disappearing into a cloud. At some times during the day clouds would pass, blocking our site of the wonderment, but the docking cloud never moved. Almost at evening, Old Man Todson was heard to yell as he came up to the crowd that lingered below the ship, "Did I not tell you? I knew they would come!"

Brand checked again with Dorena, and again she nodded. He moved to the next entry. "What we write here we decree is true. A man appeared next to Old Man Tremor, suddenly before our eyes as if out of the air. Without looking at us, he smiled at the old man and told him he was glad to see him again. He asked if he was ready and Old Man Tremor had time to nod only once and he disappeared from us. He was gone. Someone yelled and soon everyone seemed to panic, some running, some yelling, and some, such as my beloved wife and I could only watch, dumbfounded. The strange man stood there a moment, looking at us, as though he was curious about us! Then a priest came forward and exclaimed that the man was a devil and had stolen the old man. When he pointed an accusing finger, the man raised his own hand palm outward and told us;

"There is no one time, or one place that can hold the Nation of the Star People." It was then that he, too, disappeared, and the flying sky ship could be seen to move with activity, first the hands moving busily about the sails, then the ship itself as it moved away, heading to the north, and disappearing behind the Bending Hills. It was soon discovered that Old Man Tremor was in his hut, in bed, wrapped in his blankets. He had died in his sleep.

Thus we concur, my wife and I, that this tale is true and witnessed with our own eyes."

Dorena smiled once more, and hugging her new husband, thanked him for doing this for her.

VALERIE 1996, Hawaii

It was a strange series of events which led me to Bridge, the Ouija board and the telling of this story. But I guess it really all began with the 'S'.

Five of us gathered the first night, all serious adults with a belief in the supernatural and the possibility that there was actually something out there for us to contact. Nobody was of a mind to pretend or joke by pushing the planchette around for thrills. It ended up being a pretty uneventful evening, the highlight being when Bridge got some movement and it produced the 'S'.

I, for one was quite disappointed; I'd read a book that gave me reason to believe that maybe there really were entities who could talk to those on earth. I wanted to believe. Bridge, instead of being disappointed, was encouraged by the "S", and she took the board home with her to practice. A few weeks later, she was getting broken sentences and misspelled words. I started getting interested again, and we started having three hour sessions a couple of times a week.

But some of it started getting kind of freaky, and I was getting worried that we might have let something in we should have been more careful about. One word of warning: if you ever try this for yourself, NEVER just ask "Is anybody out there?"

What I learned in those first few months, was that this stuff is real, and powerful, and not something to be considered a toy or a game. I read a few books, and figured out that I needed to write a statement of intent, complete with a precise list of rules that any entities answering would have to abide by, such as only speaking truth, no misleading statements, a good sense of humor, good past life associations, etc etc. I was pretty specific; and come to find out later, that is always your best protection. They MUST follow your rules. Nothing is allowed without your permission, either expressed or implied. Keep that in mind if it ever gets scary. You can always say no, or go away.

So anyhow, after a rocky start and some questionable information over a few months, we got back on track. I actually interviewed three entities and we chose the one who was the clearest. Once we met Olak, who had last lived in 91 BC, dying at the young age of sixteen in a Roman cell, it had become obvious that there was something to this whole experience. Predictions came true, references checked out, and we were both convinced we really had contacted a teaching spirit.

I became fascinated by my many past lives; a lot of the time when I had Bridge and the board available, I had questions involving reincarnation. I learned I'd been a wig-maker who wouldn't ever let his own family cut their hair; I'd made shoes in Egypt with Bridget, and I'd once been the wine taster for the

Marahaja of a Persian caravan. One was quite fascinating, when I had been an Plains Indian hunter and white-buffalo-tracker; but that's a subject for a book onto itself.

The story that really began it all, started with a question about an old boyfriend who had recently written after several years. I asked to be told a story about the most important lifetime that David and I had ever shared, as a birthday gift. Little did we know the telling of this tale would take 10 years to complete, and was only the start of a whole series of books. In fact, we had no way of knowing at the time, but this was actually the third tale chronologically, although for us, it was the first.

This is that story.

WESTLY 1694, London

When you were but a lad, many lives before this one, your father was a sailor. He traveled to foreign lands, a feat that took many years in those days, and much time was spent waiting to see his ship appear on the horizon. But finally the time came when neither ship nor sailor returned, and your mother was certain that your had father perished in a storm at sea. You were not so willing to suppose that your father was dead. Secretly you believed that he was living far away, happily enjoying a new life, with a new wife; and you were right, although you never knew it.

You grew into a strong young man in England, which was not easy at the change of the 18th century; especially in the home of a poor sea-widow. Now forced to work for the churches that would have her, as a charwoman, you watched as she was paid weekly in small black potatoes and moldy bread, while the clergy grew fat on donations meant for orphans, such as you. You were witness to the marvels of the burgeoning Age of Information, and the introductions of multitudes of new inventions, seemingly on a daily basis. And while all of this potential and expression of the human race was revealed to you, you were also privy, most personally, to the poverty that was allowed, and the glaringly unfair distribution of wealth that marked this island kingdom. You realized from a young age that there would be no opportunities for you here, no chance for anything different. It seemed that if you were to work at all, you would have to be just like your father, a sailor. You did not blame him for leaving this place; in fact, a part of you admired it.

You gave help to your mother when you could, but for each job for which you applied, there were dozens of boys equally desperate to help their mothers, and so as soon as a place opened on a ship, you took it. It was not until you had said your goodbyes to your mother, and stowed your meager belongings that you inquired from the captain as to your destination. It was an old Moorish trader and it was headed for the growing British colonies in the New World. Your first voyage among the high seas was much like your feelings concerning the world; clouded and stormy, and your only goal was to experience the world on your own terms, without regret or fear of consequence.

Even as young as you were, you learned all there was to learn about ocean sailing on that trip, eager always to take a crew-member's place, so that you would have all the more knowledge of that post. But no amount of training could help when a great storm blew upon the ship with such force that the crew expected to perish, and sent the ship far to the north. Badly broken, the ship limped into the cold harbor known then to most simply as Ottawa. Tucked within the protective confines of the Gulf of St. Lawrence, it was an ancient fishing village, now shared by Colonists and Natives alike, though there were various companies trading in furs who had laid claim to the area. One of the larger companies had claimed this harbor, and a modest yet comfortable manor had been built not far away for the Harbor Master.

Wallace Young enjoyed his title, "Master of the Ottawa Fleet", and he was more than happy to extend his harbor's hospitality to your ship while it made repairs. As for captain and crew, he invited them to visit him at his manor as they would, and pass the time regaling together their many sea adventures. As the ship was badly damaged, it soon became clear it would take weeks or even months before you could hope to sail again.

Some months had passed this way, when one restless evening you found yourself walking alone near the manor, trying to think of a way that you might get to the next village up the coast. It was reported to have whiskey, and while you were not much of a drinking man; it was more the idea of escaping boredom than anything that appealed to you. You knew that if you could just get a hold of one of the smaller ships, you could take her out, get to the village and back again before anyone would miss her. The problem would be getting passed the sentry at the wooden watchtower.

These were the thoughts you were thinking when you saw Talia, the harbor master's young new wife. Wallace Young was a proud man, and paraded his newest acquisition whenever given the chance. She was clearly very young, and you could see that there was some Native blood in her, and while her husband harshly ordered her about you could see that she still had spirit in her. She was kind to all the sailors, and carefully looked over the kitchens, making sure that the visiting crew was given extra to eat, since they were not used to the northern climes. That was why, when you saw her walking alone, you did not hesitate to wish her a good evening. When she asked how you were faring, it suddenly occurred to you to tell her the truth, exactly. You admitted your intense boredom with her land, and how you wished to borrow a ship and why. You recalled that she earlier had been disappointed that their store of venison had been raided by rodents, and you reminded her that the next village would most likely have more of that meat available, in addition to the whiskey. You offered to bring her some.

Talia smiled at your request, and the honesty in which it was made. She admitted that she too was bored of her own land and told you of her envy of you and your "windswept ways". You could see that she meant what she said. Then, looking with anger at the manor's walls, she suddenly agreed to help you. Had either of you foreseen the ensuing events that would be brought about by this decision, neither may have had to courage to proceed.

She held her head high as she led you to the water, and you could see that she was not the least bit afraid. The light of a full moon lit your way as you walked, and you smiled when she declared that this was her time to do something daring, for a change. You knew she was referring to her new husband, gone as he was much of the time on business for the giant company that built this place. Glancing about at the dense forest and frigid waters that made up this river harbor, you could not blame her. In fact, you admired her; such audacity was rare in a woman in those days; a wife could be sent to prison by her husband's words alone. And she was clearly part native, on her mother's side you assumed, since there were no white women hardy enough to survive the winters in this land.

Never idle during these months, you had traveled as you could on foot, meeting with the other sailors and through them spending time talking, sharing drink and gambling with the many native peoples that came to trade fish and furs with the Europeans, all along the river. It was there you discovered that you could buy your own wife very cheaply, and it was considered no dishonor on either side. If you were dissatisfied, it was fine to sell her to another or back to the tribe; the only rule was that you could not kill her. As you followed Talia down the boardwalk to the watchtower you wondered in awe how such a young beautiful creature as her could stand so tall and sure, in the midst of such a life.

The watchtower was not tall; it was meant only to watch the ships, with only one of the company's soldiers to man it. He stood close to his brazier to stay warm, until the harbor master's wife walked in, when he snapped to attention. Without hesitating, Talia explained that her husband was ill, and had sent her to relay his orders. Seeming the caring wife, she explained how she had convinced her suffering husband that she could succor relief for him in the potion of a neighboring tribe, if only someone could be sent. She told him he had chosen you for the job and she gestured toward the small schooner you had indicated as the one you hoped to borrow. Taking into account that you had spent some months under the care of the Wallace Young, it was no surprise that the soldier took you as one of the company's crew. Talia was entirely convincing in her distress for her husband, and the man wasted no time in signing the log book stating that the Harbor Master himself had ordered the commissioning of the ship.

Talia followed you to the dock, reminding you with a pleasant laugh not to forget the venison you had promised. Her smile was radiant in the moonlight and you could see she was clearly please with what she had done.

"Come with me." You said it suddenly, for it had occurred to you suddenly; perhaps she too might want to escape her circumstances, if only for a small time. You truthfully assured her that she could be back before first light. To your delight, she showed her assent by boarding the ship.

You had never sailed on your own before, and while it was difficult at first, you mastered it quickly. Such challenges always seemed as games to you, and this was no different; you knew what needed to be done and you did it. The only trick was not to quit, ever. Once underway, the current of the deep river did the rest.

The sky was clear, and once free of the smoke from the fires of the crowded harbor and its village, the stars shone brilliantly. Rarely allowed to leave the manor, Talia had not seen the stars so bright in all of her memory. You stood on the deck with her, as she gazed in wonder, remarking upon their beauty. You traded stories of the different explanations for what the stars were. Talia told of how her mother thought they were campfires of other tribes, in the distance. You told her of the latest idea in Europe, that stars were balls of fire, like the sun. Talia replied that a bowl of fire would make more sense, since it would explain night, an image that caused both of you to laugh. You briefly discussed the opinion of the Christian Bible, that the stars were simply markers to help separate the heavens from the firmament, and it became clear quickly that neither of you cared for the doctrine, though each had been raised with it. Running out of stories, each of you decided that none of the known theories could explain the beauty and variation they were witnessing, nor the affect it inspired in them as they stood there. At one point Talia ask you what you thought they were. You had an idea, but in an effort to hedge your time, you asked her the same question in return. She admitted that she did not know, though she wished she did. Lost within your thoughts, you both grew silent for a moment, each of you thinking of the sparkling star field that was laid out across the sky. You wanted to tell her what you thought about the stars, for you had an opinion indeed, but you were not used to sharing your opinions with anyone. This was especially true if it meant anything to you, and this did. But here she was, this incredible young woman who should probably still be tending her mother as a maiden, willing to take charge of her own life, if only for a brief time. This exquisite creature was standing next to you, of all people, asking your opinion of the stars…

"I believe people live among those stars," you declared, and it was like a sort of music, an echo deep within your soul, as you heard Talia say the same words, at the exact same moment.

You could see that she was as surprised at your words as you had been of hers, and that she believed those words. Looking at her now, so happy and free, you felt you could share anything with this woman. You asked her again, playfully, if she really did believe that people lived among the stars and when she most heartily insisted that she did, you told her that you had seen evidence that such things were true. Except as a child at your mother's knee, you had never discussed this with anyone; nor had you ever thought that you would see the day when you would.

Briefly, you told Talia of your upbringing in England, and of how your mother raised you alone. "She has one possession," you related, and explained that it was a family Bible, purchased by your great, great, grandparents, Brand and Dorena. It had been passed down to her from her mother, and then from her mother. You told Talia of the strange thing written in the section of the book where births and deaths are recorded. "It was clearly written by my great, great grandfather, but he chose to write it a few pages further in the book. My mother found it because it was written directly in the birth entry where my name would have gone. Instead, she had to record my name even further within the pages." Then you told what was written there; the story of when your ancestors actually met people from the stars.

"There was an old man in that village that everyone thought was crazy, because he insisted people lived among the stars. Until one day when a three-masted ship, fully rigged and with a full crew, appeared in the sky, and docked at a cloud." You waited to hear her response, expecting an objection and were pleasantly disappointed when she replied thoughtfully,

"I have not ever thought about it, but I imagine they would have to dock at a cloud." Then, eagerly, she asked you to continue.

"They came to that very village to retrieve that same crazy old man. It turns out that he was one of them. A man appeared out of thin air, and he knew the old man, just as a brother knows a brother. He asked him if he was ready and when the old man said he was, the old man disappeared, just as mysteriously and utterly as the Starman had appeared. The village almost came to blows with the stranger, suspecting him of being with the Devil. It was here that the man spoke to the angry villagers." You noticed that Talia moved closer, hanging on your every word, "He told them that there was no one time and no one place that could hold the Nation of the Starpeople. Then he too disappeared and within a small while, the ship undocked and sailed through the sky from their view, to the north."

"The Starpeople..." Talia repeated dreamily

when you had ended. "I like that." A moment later she added, conviction in her voice, "I believe your great, great grandparents."

You smiled, "So do I. I think they will come for me when my time comes, just as they did back then."

The idea clearly pleased her, and she told him that she too would like to meet the Starpeople someday. You watched as she stood there on the deck, looking up into the star-studded sky, smiling at the idea, and you were glad that you had shared your most important secret with her. By sharing it, you knew you had given her the same hope that Dorena and Brand had given you. Perhaps, you thought, it would help her when you returned her to the cold harbor, and back to her cold husband.

Again, you could see, even feel, the unfairness of the situation. It did not make sense that this beautiful woman, so imaginative and open-minded, was forced against her will to live in this rugged land, locked in by ice in the winter, and by her mockery of a marriage every second of the day. With out thinking you asked aloud, "How can you live in such isolation as this?" You were answered, to your own dismay, by her tears. Rather die than see her so pained, you instinctively reached out and hugged her to you.

You said nothing more for a time, allowing her to cry until she was spent, and then you simply held her as she slowly calmed down. You realized that she had probably not cried since her marriage, brave as she had tried to be as the wife of Wallace Young. The thought of returning her to that overbearing oaf was now appalling to you, and you knew that you would have to try to help her.

"Would you like to meet the Starpeople?" you asked her, pointing to the North Star of the Little Dipper, and when she nodded, you told her that you would arrange it. This made her smile, which eased your heart, and she asked how you purposed to meet the people who lived among the stars. You assured her that you would know when the time came, and if need be, you would meet them halfway. As long as she wished it, it would be so. "You have heard what happens when one believes," you told her, "imagine how much easier for the Starpeople to find us when there are two who believe!"

She watched you for a moment; you knew she was weighing the sincerity of your words, and while her eyes were serious, the smile never left her.

"I did not know of the Starpeople," she said finally, "but I believe you, Westly."

And so you were decided. Once you came to you the tremendous mouth of the river, you did not head to the village to the north, but instead turned the ship south, and into the open seas.

Steadily making progress toward Florida, a month went by while Talia and you learned more about the other. Each day was a small and wonderful adventure as you taught Talia the workings of the ship, and the fine points of sailing it. Always eager, she was a quick learner and daily she told you of her happiness to be away from her old life. You thought she was beautiful from the day you saw her; now that she had her freedom she was even more so. Nor did she waste that freedom. Often, and without warning you would find her suddenly wrapping her arms around you, hugging you closely. You returned her affection in kind, careful not to press her. It was soon, however, that she made it clear that she trusted you with everything; her new found freedom, her thoughts and feelings, and even her body.

Through the ocean you made good time with your limited crew; you had to. Though you did not mention it to Talia, you daily looked northward for pursuit, knowing that it was just a matter of time. When you docked near the Keys of Florida you discovered that you were already a wanted man. You almost could not believe your luck. It was no surprise that a fully manned ship from Canada could beat you to Florida, but it was a miracle that you and Talia had not been spotted when they passed. Silently you gave thanks to the Starpeople, wondering if they had anything to do with such fantastic fortune.

Going upon shore for supplies, you overheard a rowdy crew of pirates, lustily discussing their next "acquisition". There was a fleet of whaling ships coming from the north, and while the rugged criminals had no use for lamp oil, they had every intention of robbing each sailor who attempted to take leave upon these islands.

It was the wrong season to follow whales

south, you knew that. You figured, correctly, that Wallace Young had looked north for his ship and his wife, since that is where the commission had listed the destination. When the harbor master had exhausted those possible hiding places and realized that you must have gone south, the man had become all the more enraged. Without waiting any further, he had gathered the largest grouping of ships he could muster at a moment's notice and headed out, himself in command. You admitted to yourself that you had not thought the harbor master would go to such great lengths to catch a thief. The cost to launch such a fleet was a hundred times more expensive than the cost of the one small schooner that you and Talia had taken, and you wondered what was in the man's mind. With a heavy heart, you knew that in order to be fair to Talia, you had to tell her.

You thought she would cry in fear, and again the young woman surprised you. Instead, she gazed north, as though she might see the fleet in the distance, she told you that she had guessed that her husband would not let her go, though she had prayed he would. Then, with a determination in her voice that you had not heard before, she insisted that she wished to return to Wallace Young. She would not hear your protests, telling you only, "I could not live if you were killed." She was so insistent that finally you could not bear to discuss it at all.

With Young's ships closing in, you fought to find a way to change Talia's mind. One late, sleepless night you stood alone upon the deck, whiskey bottle in your hand. You were not trying to get drunk, but only relax, maybe enough to figure something out that would allow you to remain together. You thought of the Starpeople, and how Talia would never meet them now; never see their billowing golden sails in the sky. Again the unfairness of the circumstances appalled you. Wallace Young had purchased his wife; you knew he had no love for Talia and he could easily purchase another. As for the ship, it did not belong to Young, but to a large company that had its own ways of dealing with thieves, through legal channels. The fact that the harbor master had bypassed those channels showed that he was not fit to command.

And Talia. You sighed as you gazed at the stars, as though they might pass your sadness along to the Starpeople. The young woman was refusing everything; she would not eat, talk, or even leave the small cabin below. She would only say that she would rather die than be the cause of your death. You had tried to cajole her, beg her, and humor her. You even came close to yelling at her. But through it all she only shook her head; her arms crossed resolutely before her, demanding to be taken to her husband. Finally, seeing her grow pale with lack of food and sun and fearing for her safety if she remained, you approached her in the dark cabin. Never could you remember doing anything so hard. Not trusting yourself to remain calm, you told her in a flat, even voice,

"Talia, I wish most for your safety. Tell me where you wish me to leave you."

Talia suggested simply that she be taken to a church with a dock. There, she told you, she would be safe while the priests sent word to her husband and she waited for the fleet. You had seen many Spanish missions along the coast, and they all looked more like prisons than houses of worship in your eyes. Most of these missions were designed to serve also as strongholds with formidable walls and locked gates; more to keep their "converts" safely within, than to keep anything out. The older ones were built from stone by slaves both native and not, and each time you had gotten close to one, you had heard the sounds of crying and moaning within. Giving Talia to one of these was almost as abhorrent to you as was giving her to Wallace Young. Finally, choosing the lesser of what seemed to you to be two evils, you turned the ship north, to St. Augustine.

It was impossible to tell who owned this city, if indeed any one country did have control of it. Seemingly a magnet to hurricanes who battered it mercilessly at least once a generation, the town proper was moved often but never far from its origin; a legacy to its tenacity. If you were to guess, you decided, you would say that it belonged to the priests. There were more churches in that one area than you had ever seen, and some were quite large. Here, you thought, at least Talia might be treated with a little more dignity.

From a village nearby you traded for a horse, using equipment you did not need from the ship as barter, and then, anchoring the ship as closely as you dared, you and Talia left in the rowboat. You did so at the first hint of light, and soon you were on your way, Talia clinging to you from behind on the fast horse. Neither of you said a word during the journey, and you were glad that she could not see your face or the tears that continually threatened to blur your vision. All too quickly you came to the place you had mapped the day before,

It was a gray building, made entirely of stone, with a thick wall of the same gray material surrounding it. The wall itself was only about five feet tall, but it was topped by a wall of wooden beams that stretched another five upward, each sharpened on the top to such a point that a bird could not have perched upon the top of it. You had chosen it, not for its location, for it was terribly close to the docks, but because of its flag. Most of these missions flew a flag or banner in much the same way a military fort did and for the same reason, to announce their affiliation. The missions had changed hands often in this land that the Spanish had named Flowers, sometimes as often as Kings and Queens had changed back in Spain. While most of the missions you had seen along this coast seemed to be of one flag, the Franciscans', this one had been different; a white background, it had a sky blue star upon it. After some inquiry, you had learned that the place belonged to the Jesuits, and though this mission was well established it was the only one belonging to that group that you had seen. The old wizened sailor whom you had asked, already half drunk as he was, had confided in you that of all the churches in this town, Catholic, Protestant or otherwise, the Jesuits were the kindest of the "…hell dogs of God" or priests.

Approaching the building from behind, you tied the horse to a tree; part of a giant grove of fruit trees unfamiliar to you. You then explained to Talia where you were and that you were now prepared to escort her to the mission's gate. But first, you asked for one more chance to change her mind. You told her you would promise her anything; she had only to name it. When she hesitated, that smile playing again in her eyes, you almost swept her up right then and there. But then again her gaze fell downward, and she shook her head, insisting once more that she would die if she were to be the cause of your death. You knew of nothing else to say, for you had already said it all on the ship. Taking her hand you kissed it, and then you led her to the gate. There you told the priests that you had found the young woman to the north of town; she had been abducted, then abandoned and now needed to contact her family and husband. They believed the story entirely, and remarking gravely over her condition, took her in. She turned once as they closed the gate, and you could see no tears upon her face. You knew that she wanted you to see that she held no regret for your time together.

You wasted no time in returning to the rowboat. You did not hurry because you feared pursuit; with the image of Talia disappearing behind the mission's walls, you did not really care what might happen to you next. Instead you were trying to crowd the memory of her from your mind; if you stayed busy, you reasoned, there would be no opportunity for you to think of her. You did not take the time to sell the horse, but left it near the place where you had purchased it. Then, knowing that the fleet would pull into St. Augustine, you turned to the taverns in the little villages that lay to the south.

Always a fast learner, you had mastered most games of chance before ever landing in the New World and your time in the Ottawa only added to your knowledge of gambling. Now you put that education to good use, as you won many games, whether cards, dice, or even the game of skill known to this village as the "Pirate's Handshake". This involved a man throwing a dagger high into the air, and betting that another could not catch it without being cut. You lost the first bet, but never again. You knew better than to win every game, however. No detail went unnoticed in this wild land and you were determined to win enough for the supplies needed to sail to the great Gulf of Mexico. Once you felt you had just more than enough, you stopped and left the village. Once you were certain that you had lost the robbers whom you knew were trying to follow, you took the part of your winnings that was extra and carefully buried it. Instead of looking for a landmark and then pacing the distance to dig a hole, you looked for a place to bury the money that would be itself the landmark. In this instance you doubled back to the village closest to St. Augustine, to the ruins of an old Spanish fort. The stone was unfamiliar to you, and you wondered if it was the coral you had heard about. It appeared, perhaps a century before, that a terrific forest fire had touched this area, for the stone blocks that marked out the foundation for the fort were still blackened in some spots, and where the fire seemed the hottest the stone actually appeared glazed, as though passed through a potter's kiln. It was at the base of one of these quarried stones that you buried your gold, against the chance that you might ever find yourself in these parts again. You felt certain it would be safe here. Though it was the habit of mankind to tear down what they had built only to use the very same stones to build something new, it was not easy to remove the stones of a foundation, especially after they have had the time to settle deep within the soil. These had done just that, and though you dug as deeply as you could manage with your dagger, you never met the end of the stone. Satisfied, you rowed to the next village to the south, and bought your provisions. Once done, there was nothing left but to reboard the ship

It was fast approaching sundown. You took her out just beyond a large sandbar, and made fast for the night. Unable to sleep, you again found yourself walking the deck, bottle of whiskey in your hand. While you would have liked the idea of drowning your mind in alcohol, it was not in your nature, though you did manage to change your mood of sadness to one approaching anger. You tried to distract yourself by thinking of your future and where you might go next. You considered taking on a crew; you had been told that the lobster fishing in Espanola in the Caribbean was beyond expectation. Or maybe you would just travel alone, to Jamaica perhaps. No one asked questions in Jamaica - ever. You realized that with the ship in your hands and your skills as a gambler you could travel for as long as you chose. The world was yours.

Taking a swig from the bottle, you felt the fire of the whiskey as it slid down your throat, and you wished you could burn the memory of Talia from you just as easily. Most of the drunks at the taverns you had just visited were doing just that; each was trying to destroy the memory of a woman. But you knew no amount of drink could do that for you. Angrily, you threw the bottle overboard, casting it from you as you might a traitor. You would have no crew, you decided firmly, for you would trust no one again but yourself. The world was indeed yours, and for that matter the sky, you reasoned. It was then that you looked upward.

The glittering beauty of the innumerable stars in the clear sky was like a hammer falling upon you.

Now that magnificence served only to remind you of Talia, and the discussion you had about the Starpeople that first night you had met. You had always wondered if it was the story from your mother's Bible that had finally convinced the young woman to accompany you. Now you questioned how the Starpeople could exist, and allow such wrongdoing as what was happening to Talia. Could they not simply use there superior skills to change the young woman's mind and rescue her? If you were of the Starpeople Nation, you decided, you would find a way. Feeling the sadness returning, you turned away from the sparkling stars, but before you did, you asked the Starpeople to stay close to the young woman, and help her if they could.

Then suddenly a feeling to see Talia, even just one more time, came upon you. This was not a simple thought or notion, but an overwhelming conviction that you had to do this. Even if you saw her only from a distance as she crossed from the mission to the dock, you knew you had to be there to witness it. A part of you warned that it was folly, but you knew you could not fight this urge.

You planned your route for returning to St. Augustine carefully. With the many months you had spent in the north, chances were that there would be plenty of men onboard the ships Young was bringing who would know your face. Though the horse you had bought was right where you had left it, happily grazing, you chose to leave it behind, and walk the two miles to the town. If no one saw you now, you reasoned, there would be no knowing where to find you later. You were not deluding yourself; with the amount of men Talia's husband was bringing, it was certain that even with his wife back Young would be willing to take the time to look for his bride's abductor while he was here.

A place was found from which you would be able watch without being noticed and there you stayed, careful of your escape route once the reunion was completed. Before, as you had escorted her from the schooner, you had hurriedly begged Talia to admit no fault and to claim that every idea of the theft had been your own, which was true enough. Finally you had physically blocked her progress until reluctantly she had given you her promise.

You could see that the fleet Wallace Young had commissioned had arrived; a total of five vessels, with his whaling ship in the lead. They were just stowing their sails and in the early light you could see the rowboats as they made their way ashore. Then you heard the heavy iron latch of the mission's thick wooden gate, as they opened their doors. Surrounded by three black robed monks, Talia appeared as an angel, standing straight with her head held high. The three dark monks led her to a small landing, where they stood, awaiting the rowboats.

Young's rowboat made the landing first, far ahead of the three others that lagged behind. Even from your concealment you could hear the harbor master yelling at his rowers for speed, and when the boat did make land, he did not wait for the tie, but jumped from the vessel and stormed ashore through the surf. The giant man came at the small party on the landing almost at a run, causing even the clergymen to take a step back at his thunderous approach. This gave you an unobstructed view of Talia, and again you found yourself thinking of how incredibly beautiful she was, and you realized you were proud of her for her bravery. She had not taken a step back with the priests. Without slowing his speed, Wallace Young rushed up to Talia, who had reached out her hands to greet him. In one fluid motion the man pushed her hands away with one hand and with the other slapped Talia across the face as a man would deliver a blow to another man. You could hear the sound as he hit her, and the force of it sent the young woman to the deck of the landing.

Then your world seemed to go into a sort of slowed motion, as in a nightmarish dream. You could see every detail before you in striking clarity, and even colors seemed more intense. While you had waited from your hiding place you thought your heart might beat from your chest, nervous as you had been. Now, if pressed, you would have said that your heart had stopped altogether at the sight you had just witnesses. Just as a gale turns into a hurricane, you felt your rage rise up within you, and you knew that if you did not act, you would die right then and there.

Without another thought you ran at the group.

Wallace had only brought three men with him, so sure the braggart was of his power. The last thing the harbor master expected was that he would be attacked, and it was this surprise that helped you most. You had noticed early that the priests each had a dagger tied to their belts, so when you reached the first monk, you used your knife to cut the dagger from the thong that held his. With this new acquisition you immediately used the monk's dagger to kill the nearest guard next to Wallace by sinking it into the man's windpipe. Even as the man fell to the ground, you took his sword from his scabbard and you then proceeded to the next guard. He had managed to pull his sword out, but gave only one parry before you disabled his arm; his blade falling useless from his hand. The third guard was ready, sword drawn, and judging by the evil smile on the man's face you knew he fully expected to best you. Without another wasted motion, you threw your dagger at him, and in your anger and rage, it landed straight into the man's heart up to the hilt. The monks fled, to your relief, and within another heartbeat you had the stolen sword pointed against Wallace Young's throat. Just one more step, you thought with satisfaction, but then Talia called to you from your side. She had risen from the hard deck and was asking you to spare Wallace Young. At first you were not certain that you had heard her correctly. Unwilling to take your eyes off the man, you shook your head, and told her that surely this man must die, but again she begged for his life.

You knew that Talia was wrong; to leave Young alive was dangerous. But too, this was her fight, and if she saw fit to spare the monster, you could not see a way to refuse her. Watching the man before you, his obese flesh shivering with fear, you leaned in a little, increasing the pressure of the blade to let the man know that you did not agree with the woman. Then you brought the blade up as though you were going to slice the older man's head from his shoulder's, but instead you turned the blade to its side, and with the flat of it, you stuck Young across the face, much like the slap he had given Talia. Your stroke had left one fine cut along his left check, certain to leave a scar.

"Will you come with me now, Talia?" you asked, taking her hand in yours. You could see she was confused by the sudden attack but there was no hesitation in her voice as she said, "I will."

Without waiting another moment, you lifted the small woman, and ran for the tree line. Once you were far enough to be hidden, you gently put Talia down. Even with the horrible bruise growing upon her cheek, and the fight she had just witnessed, she was still beautiful. After determining that she was not hurt any more than that mark upon her face, you told her about your escape route, an animal path not far away. You both made your way through the heavy brush toward the narrow path, stopping often to listen for pursuit. At one point you could hear Young's voice as he bellowed his rage, and though you were too far to hear his words, you knew they were directed at you.

Twice you were forced to hide as Young's men passed closed by, but they were searching mostly from the horse trail, and never came close to seeing you. Finally you made your way to the horse, still standing there, quietly grazing. The animal had everything it could want here, and had found no reason to leave, until now as it willingly sped you along. Soon you both were in the rowboat, heading for the schooner. Once aboard the ship, you did not have to tell Talia; she immediately joined you in readying the vessel for departure.

You headed to the Caribbean, and the islands of Espanola. You were careful to keep your distance from the populated islands; you wanted no reports to get back to Young. Instead you found a small deserted island, and just to the east of it you weighed anchor. Your plan was to wait here while the harbor master and his men searched for you and Talia. Young would be watching the towns; he did not know how well you had supplied the ship .Two months passed this way, and never did you see a ship sail before the island. Soon, you both felt that you could relax, if only for a moment.

You did not waste this time with Talia. In a way you each had to learn about the other all over again, so changed by the experience as you both were. You had never killed a man before; now that you had killed two, you wondered at your lack of remorse.

Seeing that it troubled you, Talia asked that you would tell her what you did feel, if not remorse. Hardly did you wish to burden her with such base thoughts as these, but when she persisted you found her willing ear to be an invaluable gift. Never had you been able to discuss your feelings in this depth with anyone.

"It was as though they were as guilty as he," you explained. "Because they did nothing when he hit you."

Placing her hand on your own, she nodded. "I knew those men, Westly. Trust me; they were just as guilty as the man for whom they worked." She went on to explain the many atrocities the harbor master had been involved in, all in the name of commerce. This included the destruction of native villages by burning their winter homes to the ground, forcing them to trade with the forts. That was why so many native people camped near the manor, she pointed out, and why her mother had been willing to marry a white man.

It was your first evening together under a clear sky since the fight when Talia asked you suddenly, "Westly, why did you return?"

You knew she was referring to that day in St. Augustine and you told her that you had decided that you had wanted to see her one more time before she left.

She shook her head, "I mean what happened to make you deiced that you had to see me one more

time?"
You were both laying back, with her in your arms,
looking up at the sky. You could not see her face, or
her expression but her tone had grown serious. "It
seems a lifetime ago already." you admitted, and then
continuing, you held her closer. "I was back on board,
and I was very angry. I was trying to get drunk. "You
chuckled, and she laughed her light musical laugh
with you, knowing how hard it was for you to drink.
Just as you had hoped that answer would satisfy her
she asked, "Why were you so angry, Westly? "

The question startled you, and you offered,
"The world often appears unfair to me, Talia, and the
fact that a man like Wallace Young is so powerful
only served to remind me of that."

"Were you not angry with me?"

The shock of her question caused you to jump
up, with her still in your arms. "No!" you exclaimed,
turning her to face you. Once you had settled her
gently to the ground, you could see that she was
serious. "Of course not," you assured her, and then
you asked her if she had thought that was why you
had returned. When she nodded you told her all of
that night, and how you had thrown the bottle of
whiskey overboard. In your attempt to allay her fears
that she was somehow guilty of something, you
related all the details of that night in consecutive
order, right until the end, when you admitted that you
had railed against the Starpeople for not rescuing her
themselves.

It was here that Talia suddenly reached out and hugged you more tightly than she had ever done before. "But don't you see, Westly?" she whispered in your ear, "they did rescue me, through you!"

Two months were spent near that small deserted island, until finally you were forced to sail for supplies. In Espanola you discovered that the Ottawa fleet had returned to the far north. While you entertained little hope that Young would simply stop looking for Talia, you knew the fact of his returning north would give you ample opportunity to fully restock the ship. You made way for the Florida Keys.

Your first destination among this stretch of islands was a rundown Spanish village that had a small yet unusually deep harbor. This place that most people called simply the "Deep" also had the distinction that it had more taverns pressed together in one place than anywhere you had seen so far in the so-called "New World". Your plan was to earn your gold gambling, like before, then further on, to a more wholesome village to buy supplies. If your luck held, you thought, you would be able to stock the ship for another two months.

With the village in sight, you decided to stay upon the open water, not liking the cast of the morning sky. The clouds had appeared odd all of the previous day as well, and you had noticed a great many birds flying above the ship, following as you sailed along the coast. This was too much like the sky

40

you had met on your way from England, the one that had all but destroyed the ship upon which you were sailing. You told this to Talia, and you both agreed to watch the sky for a day, and make for shore upon the next dawn. The winds began before night fall, and you both worked quickly to secure anything that might blow away. Finally sure that you had done all that you could, you both retired to the cabin below.

It was well into the night when the blowing wind began to gust into angry fits that rocked the boat and sent various items in the cabin crashing to the floor. The safest place was the captain's bunk, and there you held Talia as the gusting wind turned into a sustained roar. Perhaps with a full crew, you thought, you might be able to do something, but then a gust hit the side of the ship so hard, you wondered if the entire vessel was going to tip over into the ocean. You knew then that there was no crew who could master a ship in this storm and you held Talia tighter. While you did not feel that your death was inevitable it was clear that you could do nothing to prevent it. It comforted you both to know that if you died this night you would meet the Starpeople together.

Daybreak seemed to drive the hurricane away, and you felt it was safe to go on deck just as it became light enough to see. While this storm had not been as long as the one you remembered from your first journey, it had been fiercer. That was why you were surprised to see that your masts had survived, though much of the rest of the deck was battered, and great sections of the railings were missing altogether. There would be a lot of work needed on the ship, you decided, but nothing that could not be repaired by you and Talia alone. It required only time. But first you knew that you would need supplies, and the gold to buy them.

Making your way to shore, it was like a nightmare slowly unfolding the closer you approached. The first obvious sign of trouble was the lack of palm trees, such a regular feature in these parts, which you realized soon enough were all laying down upon their sides. The few trees you had thought you saw standing you soon realized were the masts of ships that had been blown far inland, some resting upon the remains of huts. Nowhere was there a ship or boat upright in the water, or a structure upon the shore which was still standing. Ocean plants covered everything as the storm had lifted the very seafloor with its force, and then sent tremendous waves that had piled down upon the town. Both humans and sea life had been caught in the same torrents of unrelenting surges and death lay all around. No place, you thought, could have been so utterly erased from a map and you heard Talia mention "Sodom and Gomorrah", the cities mentioned in the Christian Bible as specifically targeted by God for destruction.

The only movement in the destroyed village seemed to be from those few boats, such as yours, that had come from the ocean to investigate. The village was empty, and you figured that the wiser portion of the population had moved inland to escape the brunt of the storm. Not knowing how the other villages along the coast might have fared, you told Talia that you wished to find what you could here in the way of supplies. You both made your way carefully through the wreckage. The fact that the harbor was so deep made it a popular one, and you came across the remains of a great whaling ship. The vessel was more damaged than most, and with it the buildings that had been caught in its path. At some time during the storm its rigging has snapped and its sail cloth unfurled directly into the face to the wind. Before the noble mast could break under the splintering force the gigantic sail caught the gale and it lifted the mighty ship off the ground. Propelling it inland, the ship became like an incredible cannon ball, thundering into ship and building alike with such velocity that the ship had broken open in two, from aft to fore. The area was clean of the many bodies you had seen strewn all about, and you realized that the storm surge must had carried them back to the sea. Grateful for that, you search here for materials to repair you own ship, such as rope, and planking and the like, while Talia looked for food supplies among the ruined huts nearby. It was then that your eye caught a glint of gold. Guessing by the rubble that you were near the captain's quarters you decided that it warranted exploring, and your curiosity was rewarded with a small chest. It had a promising weight to it and you put it with the other things you had collected. The villagers were sure to be on their way and you hoped to be gone by the time they arrived so you decided you would open it back on the ship, with Talia.

While you had found more than enough supplies among the wreckage of the storm to repair any damage your ship had sustained, finding food had been a challenge. Staying as long as you dared along the battered shore, your combined efforts had found enough provisions for perhaps an uncomfortable week at the most and that consisted almost entirely of the barrels of hard biscuits that long-voyage ships used as bread. Depending on the severity of the storm further along the coast, it concerned you that you might be forced to sail further north than you would do otherwise.

You had guessed that the shattered whaling ship, like most of the vessels that plied these waters was either commissioned or outright owned by the Spanish. That mighty country had claimed massive sections of the new world; their borders growing steadily for two hundred years. They had been pressing their way northward that entire time. The Spanish were a people who loved ornamentation and the more important an object, the more decorated they tended to create it. As you looked at the small chest you became certain that it contained something valuable.

The chest was not large; only the size of a loaf of bread, but it was highly worked. Wonderful shapes of flowers and vines had been artistically carved into the wood panels that made up the sides, and the lid sported a scene of various birds who all seemed about to drink of the nectar of the climbing flowers. It was held together by cleverly worked brass brackets, worked to look also like vines curling along the edges, all to meet at the clasp for the lock; again brass worked to look like two over-lapping leaves. It was not ostentatious, or flashy. Its beauty came most, you decided, not by what had been added or embellished upon it, but by how it showed itself as the only decoration. Much like Talia, you reflected as you called for her to see it.

You had kept it as a surprised, carefully hiding it until the rowboat had been unloaded and stowed. The day was fair, and you both sat upon the deck, the chest between you. At first Talia had stopped you from smashing the lock, so unwilling she was to damage the box; but when you assured you that your aim was good, and that the chest would be safe, she allowed you to proceed.

The lock, like the box, was small; there was no room for anything bigger, and it opened easily with the blow from your dagger's hilt.

Once the broken lock was removed, you asked Talia to open it, and were pleasantly surprised by her strange reaction. She was clearly stunned. She slowly put her hand out to open the clasp, but then suddenly pulled it back and asked what you thought was in it. You playfully assured her that you did not know, working hard to contain both your excitement and wonder at her hesitation. "Why do you not open it?" you asked her.

She laughed in her musical way, but you could hear a certain nervousness within the sound this time. "It is because of the box." she told you, explaining that among her mother's people, traditionally dangerous things were wrapped within beautiful packages, to recognize and celebrate the intense power of the object. As wonderful as the chest was, she reasoned, it must be very dangerous indeed. Assuring her that Europeans held no such belief, you admitted that you suspected the box might be harboring some gold. Again you were surprised when your explanation only seemed to add to her confusion.

Then you realized that she did not know the value of gold. Her life had been spent among the fur and fish traders of the cold north and her miser husband had spent no money upon his young wife. She had mentioned to you earlier that she had never owned anything, but you only now realized just what that had meant. It was so typical, you noted; to control a person by keeping them ignorant and mentally you vowed that you would teach her to master the tricky waters of banking as you had helped her to master sailing. Smiling, you gently pushed the chest toward her. "This chest and all it contains, Talia, is yours. Open it."

She looked deeply into your eyes for a moment

and you could see her nervousness disappear as her expression changed from one of doubt to one of trust. She opened the chest.

It was gold, all of it. Talia pulled out coin after coin of Spanish press, until she grew impatient and pulled them out by the handful. The amount went beyond anything you had thought possible, and you realized then why this decorated chest had been in the personal collection of the ship's captain. Most likely it had been headed for the king of Spain himself, and was hidden upon the whaling ship; a common practice in an area of the world fraught with thieves and pirates.

Talia had wished to remove the coins quickly because she had seen other shapes nearer to the bottom of the chest. Soon she was bringing out pieces of jewelry, as well as dozens of golden beads of different designs. With each of these she briefly paused, taking a moment to look closely as each one, then carefully placing them in a wooden bowl she had for the purpose, so they would not roll about.

Unlike Talia, you were very aware of the value of what you had found. For a moment you were in a kind of happy daze; you suddenly recalled every boyhood fancy you had ever entertained of how you would spend a fortune should one fall in your lap. Then you realized that each scheme you had concocted in the past had involved different ways of winning a beautiful woman's heart. You glanced at Talia, radiant in her intense focus upon a group of golden beads. You knew that you had already won her heart, and with nothing but yourself.

Then you noticed the dates of the coins. They were all of the famous Royal stamp, dated from the year before, and each in perfect condition. Usually bits of metal were shaved from coins and weighed as a form of payment; it was rare in the New World to see a coin with its original shape. It took you a moment to realize why these new coins were in the same chest with a collection of jewelry; the beads and jewelry were examples of the work that had been melted down into the coins, probably for easier transport back to Spain.

Talia was now pulling out strands of small golden beads perhaps half a dozen in all. Then, resting at the bottom was a necklace of golden bees. Set wingtip to wingtip, each was about the size of your small fingernail and was actually a bead strung together so that each insect was looking upward, toward the wearer. Talia was obviously entranced by it, and you let her show you the intricate detail, and how cleverly the bees lay about the string, as they might sit about their queen in their home at the hive.

The workmanship of the beads was extraordinary in that they lay perfectly about in a circle as you place the necklace around Talia's neck. Considering the dozens of beads necessary to make it, the necklace was not heavy; the bees were hollow. Their shape caused the sunlight to glint about them in such a way that they appeared to move about as Talia did, fluttering their little wings.

As Talia turned her attention to the collection of beads she had put in the bowl, you looked more closely at the now empty chest. Lined with red felt, you carefully examined the panels until you found what you were looking for. A small seam appeared down the middle of the bottom panel; you would not have noticed it had you not been feeling for it. With a dagger you gingerly pried along the edges and you were rewarded when the panel sprung up, folding in the middle and revealing a thin compartment hidden underneath. It was empty, which in light of the small pile of treasure before you was no disappointment; though it pleased you greatly that you had found out the chest's secret. Without Talia's notice you quickly placed three of the gold coins in the compartment and then pressed the panel down, closing it.

While you had been busy with the chest, Talia spread her skirt before her on the deck and was using it to hold the sculpted beads. As she would carefully examine one, she would place it back into the bowl. As she did so, you picked each up to look at. They were of various sizes and shapes; some were suggestive, such as round ones with a hint of eyes, nose and mouth of a human or other being. Of those resembling humans, some of the metal beads were so intricate in their detail, you were certain that they were modeled after real individuals. They were the faces of natives, though not of any tribe you or Talia had ever seen. Many had skulls that were almost pointed. A few were more monster than human, with fanged teeth or snakes crawling from the corners of their mouths. Besides the human faces, there were also beads representing animals. There were a few lizards, a crocodile standing on its hands and one that looked like a wild pig of some kind; but by far the majority of the unstrung beads were in the shape of various insects. Spiders, ants, moths, and even a caterpillar; you wondered at such a strange collection. Clearly the captain of the doomed whaling ship was transporting not just a bounty of gold for his king, but an art collection. You had never seen workmanship such as this, not even in the incredible work coming from France during this time.

The gold of the Spaniards was legendary. Not a week went by growing up in poverty stricken England when you did not hear someone complain about the luck of that country in their possession of the New World. Britain, like all of Europe knew from where Spain drew its tremendous strength; the gold they had found waiting for them. Not since the dark depths of Africa had such a wealth of precious metals flooded into the "Civilized World". But by the time you were born, the shipments of gold had started to dwindle and most of the bullion came from mining operations that the Spaniards paid enterprising individuals to operate, using local slave labor. It was rare anymore to hear of a new source of pre-conquest metals being found. You had heard about the natural gold and silver deposits being worked by the thousands of African slaves in the Middle Americas, but you did not think this exquisite collection came from those parts. Determined to someday discover their origin, you place two beads in your waistcoat pocked; an ant and one of the human faces. The latter bead, about the size of a large pea, was in the shape of a man's head; bald and rounded, he was thick lipped with one of those snakes peaking out of the left side of his mouth. His nose was hooked, and he had thick octagonal disks surrounding his eyes. These beads were solid and a hole was formed where the ears would be. The ant was also solid, smaller by half than the other bead, and the antenna hooked around for the string to pass through, like a charm, as was the case with most of the insect shapes.

Two years passed you as though they had been but a day. From that moment upon the deck, discovering just how wealthy you both had just become, you had told Talia that you would take her anywhere she wished to go. Thinking that you could not be more pleased with her, she told you seriously: "I wish to see everything there is for us to see." So, to grant her wish, you had plotted always onward, toward port or place that neither of you had been before. How long you remained at any one spot depended only upon her word. She was fascinated with the seemingly endless diversity among the local natives as you both sailed about the Caribbean and you would sometimes find yourself a month or more in one location while Talia would trade and attempt to communicate with the locals. Though her hazel eyes were round and her nose the slightly upturned petite form of the French, her skin was darker than a European and her long thick hair was the raven black of an American Indian. Everywhere locals accepted her as a friend often before being introduced and her natural friendliness had come in handy many times, especially when looking to find a fair trade for the gold beads. Towns with Europeans she shunned, though she was treated equally well there. She could almost be called short, but she stood so straight, and was always so attentive to whatever she was dealing with, Talia seemed tall. Her mother had been careful to show her how to behave in white society; the best she could hope for her daughter and you were impressed to see how well she held her own when she was forced into the bigger towns. But she did not like European society, she discovered. As far as she was concerned it was no better than society in the far north where she had been born, only greener and warmer.

As for yourself, you had once harbored the notion that if ever given the chance, you would join a guild. Since you had never came close before to having the enormous fees to apply, you had never considered which guild you might wish to join. Unlike the old days, a person did not have to make a guild art his life's work, but anyone willing to pay dues could join. Now that you had the means you found that the idea of a guild had also been yet another way to attract a woman's heart. You abandoned the plot entirely; daily Talia reminded you of her love in words and deeds. You were well satisfied with being the captain of the ship, and almost daily you added to the sea charts, as well as the land maps. Since you both did well at drawing, you had started a journal of local edible plants to accompany the various charts you were creating. Though your early attempts at illustrating were childish at best, you both were showing enough progress to encourage you to keep the project going. Besides these endeavors you both spent time continuing your education, eagerly snatching books as they made their way slowly south from the giant new presses in New England colonies. Each book seemed to bring some new branch of science to light, and you would read to each other, sometimes stopping to discuss the merit of various ideas.

Staying toward the south you sailed as the whim took you and the weather warranted. Taking on no cargo but the provisions for two, your ship was always light enough to outdistance any ship you spotted that sported a British flag. It became a habit of yours to take care of where you docked, and how quickly you might leave, should there be a need. But never did such a need arise. The danger that you had hoped to avoid had not come from a British flag, though the person who betrayed you was in fact a countryman. Unbeknownst to you an acquaintance from your time in Ottawa, Lap Jackson, had seen and recognized Talia. No one would have known the ship you had taken so long ago as the one you sailed now; the hurricane and you subsequent repairs had seen to that.

Jackson also had abandoned the cold north and was now a sailor upon a dark-hulled flagless ship transporting hundreds of slaves to the burgeoning plantations of the Caribbean. While bearing you no ill will, seeing Wallace Young's wife was the biggest stroke of luck Lap Jackson had ever experienced. The old sailor had not forgotten the rage the harbor master exhibited upon the return to his manor those two years before. Young had stayed drunk for more than a month, refusing to leave his private chambers until the wound upon his face had healed completely. The company offered the usual reward for the capture of pirates, and the return of their ship. The sad fact was that all ships were fair game on this Eastern Seaboard. The most common law in these waters was piracy, and that occurred on all sides. Losing a small schooner barely registered in the annals of the bookkeepers back in England. But Wallace himself had upped the ante; he had offered a large reward with his private funds for any information about his wife, or the rogue that had stolen her. Each year only seemed to remind the harbor master of his loss, and each year he had added to the reward. Realizing that his knowledge was more valuable than his pay as a sailor, Jackson had jumped ship for the first boat back to Ottawa. Now Wallace Young not only knew your whereabouts, he also had a recent description of the ship. None of this was known to you.

There was a village where Talia made such good friends of the women there, they would meet her at first light, while it was still cool, to escort her to their homes. This was one of the few free local towns left among the islands. This was mainly because there was nothing of value upon the land and no draft deep enough for the large cargo ships that plied these waters. There was a fishing village on the lee side of the island, and a small town of huts further inland. A person could walk twice around the island in a day. The locals were shy and quiet, though once they got to know a person they considered them family, and they had all but adopted you and Talia as their own. The women of the town were learning how to sew from Talia and in return they were sharing their knowledge of the native herbs and plants, and all were eager for each day's lesson.

Talia would rise early, while it was still dark and be ready to row ashore as soon as it was light enough for her to manage. She had insisted that there was no need for you to accompany her, since she had at least a dozen helpful women waiting upon the shore for her. In fact, Talia had a way of moving about so silently that she could prevent you from waking altogether, if she so desired. But never did she go anywhere, even if only for a few minutes, without first kissing you.

Such was the case early one morning, when Lap Jackson, knowing he would now be receiving that reward, happily pointed to the ship where you lay sleeping. At first Wallace Young did not recognize the schooner, so well had you hidden her features, but as they drew closer, he nodded grimly. With almost a growl he gave the orders to load the cannon.

It would be some days before you could piece together all of the events of that morning. Many of the details were provided by the men working in the fishing village. After Talia's departure, you returned to sleep in the cabin, which was still so dark that you knew it was not yet dawn. After some time you were awakened to the very world exploding around you. Although you had never experienced war, you knew the sound of cannon. Even as the wood of the ship burst under the blow of one shot, you could hear the report of the next one being fired from nearby. The air became a mixture of fire and smoke, seawater and broken wood as cannonball after cannonball rained down upon the small ship, or cut through it from the side and tearing open great sections of the decks below.

It was the shape and position of the captain's berth that saved you. Being carved from a single piece of dark hardwood, it was like a large three-sided box lined on the bottom with a thick down mattress. The whole affair was set into the side of the ship that was facing away from the sudden assault. When the first cannon had been fired, the metal ball had ripped through the side of the galley, and sent the greater portion of that room's furnishings and fixtures careening onto the berth where you lay. The wooden bed frame held without breaking, and during the rest of the attack you were tossed mercilessly about in what you ironically thought would be your coffin. Finally one cannonball hit so closely that you were dragged below the water with it and your protective enclosure was lost to you. Blindly, you made your way through the flotsam to the surface. There was no lack of planks in the water to buoy you, and you held on, trying to see through the smoke. The air was quiet now, and you could hear orders being shouted in the distance, though you could not make out the words. So you remained quietly gripping the small plank until you could hear the ship depart, and could no longer hear the voices. Slowly making your way towards shore, you did not see anything worth saving. Talia was safely upon land, and the gold; you had buried the gold on the island. When ever you knew you would be long in one place that is what you did. With just the two of you, the ship was often left unguarded, so burying the gold collection had long become a habit for you. The charts and maps were a heavy loss to you, especially the fair drawings that you and Talia had made. But mostly it was the loss of the ship itself that bothered you. You could have purchased a new one long ago with the gold, but instead you had changed it just enough to be unrecognizable. You and Talia had met on that ship;

you had loved and live, and you had reinvented yourselves there. And now it was gone forever.

The word in the village was that a restored Dutch warship, with twenty cannons at least, had sailed around the island the evening before, and had returned at dawn that morning. The men had watched from the beach in angry surprise as the frigate raised a black flag, and made for the schooner, anchored alone in the deeper water beyond the surf. Within moments their surprise had turned to horror as they watched the Dutch ship's cannon rolled forward and ignited. An island of kind and generous people, the senselessness of the onslaught was appalling to them. Even after seeing you alive and whole, they would not stop patting you on the back, so impressed they were by your survival of the attack they had just witnessed.

Talia had heard the continuous thunder of the cannon, and had raced to the beach, fearing the worst. You were thankful to reach her on the trail, before she could see the remains of the destroyed vessel, floating in pieces on the water. You wanted to tell her yourself, to assure her that everything would be alright, and that you could both get a new ship, and you could rebuild your lives, draw again those plants, and get new books and remake the charts and maps. But she did not even ask about those things. Instead she hugged you to assure herself that you were alive and well, then she insisted that you sit right where you were with her on the trail, where she could hold you. And there you stayed for the rest of that day, while the thoughtful villagers occasionally brought food and water.

The villagers never asked you questions concerning that morning, though they did have plenty to say about it. They spoke of the attack as though they were discussing strangers instead of you and Talia, their good friends. This was true even when they were standing right before you.

"Those pirates wanted to kill that poor young couple and kill them they did." they remarked.

"Do you see the wreck? Who could survive such a thing?" they asked each other and the answer was always the same, said with pretended sadness, "Those pirates will never see that young couple again."

Soon it became clear that in the future telling, the villagers would add the detail of your deaths when telling the story of the great pirate attack that had occurred in their small lagoon. It was clear that whatever you might have done to warrant such an attack, it had not affected their good judgment of you.

But once alone in the hut that the natives had generously provided for your use, Talia had questions. Both of you knew that the attack had been from Wallace Young, but the young woman did not understand why he attacked the way he did, instead of simply turning you in as thieves. And she wanted to know why he had not stayed to make sure he had succeeded, as hell-bent as he had seemed to be to destroy them. They were all good questions, and you told her so. While you could prove nothing, you had your ideas and shared them with her. You agreed that you would never have imagined that Young would have taken the pirate's route. Had the man been caught under the banner of a black flag, he would have been hung from that very ship's yardarm. However it had happened that he had found you, the British overlords of the harbor master's company must not have been willing to finance a sudden foray south. This forced Wallace Young to hire a flagless ship instead. It pleased you to you think of the fortune he must have spent on such a heavily loaded rig, though you did not let Talia know this. She did not understand Young's incredible anger, and she was still deeply disturbed by the intensity of the attack. But you understood the older man's actions. You knew it had nothing to do with the ship you had taken, or even Talia herself for that matter. This was about the embarrassment the man had experienced at being bested by a single man, and a man young enough to be his son. You knew that you could have stolen a bottle of wine from the old braggart and he would have reacted with the same ire; though maybe not with the same amount of firepower. Wallace Young was a man who would allow no mark to besmirch his name, and would allow no amount of time to dull his sense of indignation. He had a list of grudges, and a person was removed from this list only by the liberating hand of his revenge. But now, with the help of the villagers, the word would go out that no one had survived the destruction of the schooner. There would be no reason for anyone to look for you now.

After recovering from the initial shock of losing all of your possessions, you and Talia began the pleasant task of starting over. The first thing to do, you both agreed, was to get another ship. There was no such thing as a good ship for sale in these island studded waters, and you booked passage for Talia and yourself on the first ship passing that was making non-stop for Florida. This turned out to be an empty cargo ship that would be filled with lumber from the north forests and carried back to the wood-poor islands of the tropics. Large estates were springing up everywhere and grass huts were no longer acceptable to the new European masters, who were reproducing the large mansions they were all too poor to afford back in their homelands.

The journey was slow, the winds not being favorable to the ship, but neither of you minded. It was the first time since you met that you were given such leisure, since daily both of you had before tended to the chores of the ship. There was no fear of pirates, since the cargo ship road high in the water, revealing she carried nothing, and the crew was jovial and even merry the entire time. By the time you were making the first port, you had many leads for finding and purchasing a good ship.

She was an older vessel, but you could see from the start that she was stout and seaworthy. You particularly liked the idea that she was accustomed to these climes; she knew her way around the Eastern Seaboard of the Atlantic Ocean. Besides, if there was a flaw in her design, you reasoned, it would have been discovered long ago.

She was a Spanish ship, refitted twice in her life, and she rested in the largest shipyard you had seen since leaving England. The honest men on the lumber ship had stopped in the grand harbor of Havana, and you found that you had to go no further, for that was where your ship lay. Like so many vessels, she was practically unrecognizable from her days as what you suspected had started as a caravel, and it was clear that she hadn't held cargo in some time. Instead she had been refitted lately as a sort of floating house for a Spanish soldier who had been granted land on a deserted island. Before that she had been a working boat for pulling logs about this long island, to the shops where the massive amount of wood products that were created here. Before that, you wondered if she had not perhaps been the ship of an explorer, which is what your plans for her were.

The docks were noisy and crowded, and Talia had remained aboard while you stood with one of a dozen harbor masters that managed Havana's busy waters. You both had been satisfied by the transaction, you for the fine ship you had just purchased, and the harbor master for the fact that you were paying in Spanish gold coins. Since taking on the job, the man had become accustomed to seeing all sorts of payment in the harbor, from sugar to human cargo. He was happy to be able to accept payment from a British man and then take his leave from you.

With the paperwork in hand, you looked to Talia on the deck to show the title to her. But her attention had been taken by the activity on the large whaling ship docked next to you. A Dutch whaling vessel, you noted, and it was busy getting ready to make sail, bustling with activity. But it was not the doings of the crew that had her attention. Instead she was intently watching two young boys as they were being scolded by a man three times their size.

Clearly a foreman by the way he ordered people about in between his swearing at the two before him, he kept his great hands balled into fists, and would punctuate his words with threatening jabs at the children. Talia would later guess them to be about seven and nine years old, and they were of a variety of native you were unfamiliar with. Traveling as you had along the coast of the new world you had seen more examples of tribes than you could ever count. Taking into consideration the generations-long campaign that the Conquistadors had begun of enslaving all of the local populations which they encountered, it would be no surprise to see members of a French speaking tribe of natives from Louisiana being sold as slaves to a Swedish speaking cattle baron in the Bahamas. But it had become rare to see natives of pure blood from the warmer areas. For reasons no one knew, they died easily under the strain of slavery, and the greatest example by far of slaves that you had seen throughout the New World had been the Africans who compromised such a large share of the cargo ships that plied these waters. Such was the case with this Dutch ship that had so captured Talia's attention; the two boys seemed to be the only natives on board at all, and they did not seem to understand the Dutch, Spanish or broken English that the man was alternately yelling at them.

You allowed your gaze to sway between Talia and the scene on the other ship. She was standing tall, her hand resting on the rigging, and she leaned forward a little. Then, when you looked at the other ship, you thought you recognized what it was that held Talia's attention; the children were not flinching under the verbal assault, just as she had not under the rule of her ruthless husband back in Ottawa. Certainly, they would move back a step when the giant fist came at them each in turn, but they never cried or looked away. The foreman was claiming that they were worthless and lazy and that he had been cheated. His job was difficult enough without having to train jungle babies who didn't know how to talk, he insisted. The man's anger grew with each moment, and it was clear that he had no wish to calm it. He reached for a thick wooden fish-club and made as though he was going to strike the taller boy, and while the smaller one closed his eyes, still they did not flinch. But the foreman had seen the younger boy's eyes close, and laughing, he struck the older boy with his open hand, causing the nine year old boy to fall hard upon the deck; then watched to see what the younger would do. The seven year old did not move, but again he closed his eyes.

You looked for Talia's reaction just as she screamed. For the briefest second you wondered at the sound, since you had never heard her express fear. She was clearly shocked, her face was ashen, her delicate eyebrows were knitted in concentration, and she was holding her hand to her face. Looking at you, she pointed off to the whaler and implored simply, "Save them!"

Calling to Talia to remain aboard the ship, you made your way through the crowded wharf to the large whaling ship. The multitude of men were busy with their own tasks and no one noticed as you approached the foreman, who was now commanding the older boy to stand up. You wasted no words and told the man that you would buy the young slaves from him. At first the man pretended that he did not understand, but after informing him that you had heard him speaking the King's English he shrugged his bear-like shoulders. Like so many of the people who populated the Netherlands, this man was huge, now only tall but broad in the upper torso. His arms were as big as many men's legs.

"The business of these is mine," he told you, then ordered you off the ship, and turned his back on you.

You were jovial with the man; truly you had

nothing against him so far. You explained how you had seen the difficulty he was having at training the two children, and how you would be willing to buy them from him. "Surely you can find better than this," you pointed out.

The giant laughed, his rotting teeth only adding to the image of a monster, "Traded them I did, cost me nothing!" The nine year old had been having difficulty clearing his head enough to get to his feet, even with the younger boy's attempt to help him. The foreman now reached down and grabbing the boy by the neck, swiftly set him on his feet. The child managed to stay standing, but was now coughing from the sudden assault to his windpipe.

"Really?" you inquired, seeing the man was obviously pleased with himself that the slaves had cost him no money. "What did you trade?"

The Norse man's eyes were shining. "Half bottle of rum, and not good rum at that! Stupid Spanish priest..." he mutter with a chuckle.

Again you offered to buy the two, and told him, "You could buy enough rum for a month if you sold them to me for gold."

When the man shook his head, you told him that you would give him twice the amount of a slave's worth if he would part with them then and there. This gave the man pause and he looked at you closely. You knew he was wondering about your motives, so you offered that you did not trust black slaves, and explained the difficulty of finding natives for sale as slaves. He seemed to be considering this when he happened to glance at your newly acquired ship and saw Talia watching. Though she was not visible crying, it was clear that she was upset by what she had witnessed. You watched with some dismay as a light seemed to grow in the slow mind of the giant, and he turned back to you, grinning slyly. He knew now why you wanted to buy the two boys.

"Times ten!" the foreman spat and you knew he meant that he would accept no less than ten times the going rate for an untrained first generation slave, which at that time in that harbor, was no less than four gold pieces. Then the brute looked up at Talia and laughed his ugly laughed at her.

You leaned into the man, knocking him with your shoulder. Though he was a good six inches taller than you, he was not ready for your maneuver, and it sent him backwards, almost toppling him. Had he not caught a railing with his hand, he would have fallen to the deck.

"Times five." you countered in a warning growl.

Now the foreman was no longer smiling. That fact that he had came so close to being knocked off his feet by an Englishman had embarrassed him more than he had thought possible, especially in front of the slaves, and the pretty girl on the ship next to them.

"Fifteen!" he said, then added quickly, "Speak again and it is thirty!"

"Scoundrel!" you called him, and then added

that he was no better than a pirate to take advantage of a woman's feelings.

The large man again shrugged, and took a few steps back, as though he were considering something new to say. You did not notice that he had used his large bulk to hide the fact that he had taken hold of a large hook, the sort of which was used to drag large fish on board. "Convince you I may still," he began, but then suddenly brought his right hand around toward you and with a shock you caught a glint of metal.

You dodged his first blow, which gave you the moment you needed to draw the sword you now wore whenever you found yourself on land. This kept the beast at a distance for a moment, but the fish hook was long, and at one point the foreman managed to make contact, hitting your neck, just at the base of your skull. He would have sunk the hook into you if he had done as he had planned, but you had deflected the thumb-sized barbs with your sword at the last moment, using the flat of it as a shield. Still, the metal shaft of the hook had hit you with great force, and it became a challenge to remain focused with the pain of it. You knew you had to act quickly, and so you switched from a position of defense to one of offense. Falling upon him with stroke after stroke from your sword, it was all he could do to defend himself with the hook. Already you had splintered the wooden handle, and it was becoming difficult for the large man to hold the shortened tool effectively. It was then that you heard the order given to "Stand down!" and you knew that it had been given by no less than a ship's captain. Not willing to let your guard down against this treacherous man, you kept your sword before you, but allowed the weight of the order to draw you back, and you gave the foreman quarter.

Only when you were sure that the giant had also followed the order and had lowered the hook did you look to see who had given the command. It was indeed the captain, accompanied by many of the crew who had obviously stopped their activities to watch the fight. The captain spent a moment speaking with various people in Dutch, and then the foreman. Then, in perfect English he asked you for your side of the story. You explained only that you wished to buy the boys for your wife, and had offered more than their worth, when the man attacked you. Obviously the information the captain had acquired from his crew agreed with you for he did not hesitate, but ordered the foreman below and told you, "The man does not own the boys."

Seeing your puzzlement, he went on to explain, "It is true, he traded a Spanish priest for them on the Mexican mainland, but he gave them to me to pay off a loan." Now he shrugged, "The loan was not large. You may purchase them at the original price, if your woman still wants them."

It was now that you noticed that Talia had arrived and was already closely inspecting your neck. Satisfied that there was no blood, she still expressed concern that there was a knot and bruising. Turning to the captain she informed him that she did indeed still wish to take the boys, and insisted it must be at the moment, since she had to return her husband to their ship and tend to his wound. It was her bearing, you were certain, that had caused the captain to grant her wish; he even invited you to see his own ship's doctor, which you gracefully declined.

For the third time you tried to rise from the bed, and the pain of the headache drove you back into the pillows that Talia had arranged around you. You could not decide what made you more frustrated; the fact that you had let that brute hit you, or the fact that he had hit you so hard, you could not get out of bed. So far you had seen little of your new ship, and while the captain's cabin was plush in the velvet fashions of the Spanish, you had already grown quite bored with it. Once Talia had done everything she could to comfort you, she turned her attention to the children. You had been happy to let yourself sleep at first, since it removed the pain, but you had woken now and the headache was no better. It seemed that light and even noise only made the effect worse. To Talia you admitted only that your neck was sore, and even now as you attempted vainly to sit up, she was not in the room. With nothing better to do you slept again, this time to wake in the morning. You felt a little better, to Talia's delight, and she brought the two boys to the cabin, to formally introduce them.

She had not been able to pronounce their names, and as they told you now, you too failed at your attempts to repeat them. Talia admitted that she had not had time to try to learn their names, and in all of the intense activity of the last day she had called them by what she thought was their ages; Nine and Seven. It turned out that they did know a little English and Spanish, but the boys did not know that Talia was using numbers, and were happy to use them as names she had given them; almost like a gift.

"Now they call each other Nine and Seven." she told you. You recommended that Talia let them keep the names, until they chose otherwise. They never did.

They were quiet children, even when they were trying to communicate, but they laughed easily, which was a constant mystery to you both, considering their brutal past. Though they had been fooling the Dutch foreman, they were not lazy, and knew much concerning the chores of a ship; at least the ones they could manage with their small size. Talia came often to the cabin, to tell you of the surprises she was discovering with the boys, especially with the ship.

By the next day, you truly did feel better, but not by much. Still, you decided you would die trying to reach the top deck, if that was what it took, so bored you were with being in bed. You were happy when the two boys intercepted you, and instead of protesting, each took an arm and helped you to reach the bridge. Though they were just children, the support had truly helped you keep your balance, and you were able to smile at Talia.

Nine and Seven seemed happy to have changed ships and owners. They had expressed their thanks in Spanish and were attentive to Talia, always quick to do as she requested. She had tried to explain to them that they were not to be considered slaves anymore, but it was clear that they did not understand.

"I do not know if they knew they were slaves to begin with." Talia whispered to you at one point.

Together Talia and you decided to stay within sight of land while you recovered. You still felt it was necessary to get your provisions in Florida, so you charted a course there. Though you might have planned the timing differently; now seemed the perfect time to sail along the great Gulf of Mexico. Once the boys were fully trained on the tasks of the ship, it would leave time for your hobby of map-making, and you would be able to chart the Gulf.

The pain of the headaches persisted, and within a few days you began to develop a fever. You supervised your small crew and helped when you could to get the ship underway, but on the fourth day after the injury you were again driven to your bed. With a fair wind you had already reached the tip of the Keys of Florida, and the ship was now making its way slowly along the Gulf's coast. The pain had become so weary to you that you no longer argued against Talia's promptings to return to bed.

This time you slept fitfully through the night, but with no rest; your mind was assailed by dreams that seemed to go on forever, one leading insanely into another. Talia would tell you later how you thrashed about, calling often for her and the Starpeople. You did not tell her all of your dreams; some you would not allow yourself to ever remember again after that night. There were even some dream memories of the Starpeople that you refrained from sharing completely with her. The visions were not bad; in fact they were incredible. At one point you were traveling with them upon their great galleys, sailing unimpeded between stars and planets, and calling any port home. You watched fascinated as the crew fought to keep control of the ship during a great storm. But instead of wind and rain, it was made of light and sound. A wave of sparkling light would curl before the ship and as the capable crew turned the front of the ship deftly into the wave, deafening sounds like the strokes of a violinist would sweep past you. Why you did not share all of these wonderful images with Talia was for two reasons: for one, many of the places the Starpeople's ships visited were vivid scenes of death; they were there to collect passengers who had died. The other reason you withheld certain visions from Talia was because it was clear in the dream that not only had you been the captain of a sailing Starship before your present life as Westly, you knew without doubt that you would soon be one again.

The scenes you did later share with her, she cherished always as treasures and she was certain that every detail you had dreamed was true. Her favorite to tell in later years was one in where the scrambled images of the fevered dreams had shifted to you and Talia aboard your new ship; the children were standing quietly nearby. There were three ships in the sky at once, all with sails of a golden material that were filled with unseen winds as the great crafts moved silently about. The lead vessel had lowered itself gently to but ten feet from the ocean swell and hung there disturbing neither water nor air. As the ship came expertly about, its captain left the bridge and approaching the railing called to you by name and complimented your choice of vessel. He was not tall, but his bearing was one you decided had to be of royalty but his manner was easy and gentlemanly. He was dark skinned; rather like the two boys Nine and Seven, and his hair was the same jet black as theirs. He bowed regally to Talia and remarked that he recognized the bee necklace upon her neck. His English was good, but laced with an accent unfamiliar to you. He explained that the necklace had been crafted by his people. With her usual grace, Talia offered at once to return the necklace to him, insisting that it would please her to know that it had been returned to its rightful owner. The captain would hear none of it. He insisted that he had never seen the necklace more lovely than upon her neck.

In your dream you asked the captain where they were from, and he explained that while he had many family members for crew upon his ship, many were from elsewhere. You could see many of them as they moved about the flying ship, and it was as the captain had said; there seemed to people of all color. They were all dressed differently, some in styles quite alien to you. As for the captain, he was wearing the uniform of an English man which he explained was because they were, at the moment, sailing an English ship. As for him and his family, they had last lived on Earth in Mexico. He explained that they would visit, but now their home was their ship, and that they traveled constantly; about the Earth and beyond, as well as back and forth through time.

Then he asked what you intended to name your ship. This you recalled first when you woke and at once called to Talia to tell her so that you would not forget. In your dream, upon the bridge of your new ship you answered the captain of the Starpeople's ship; you told him you named her Angel Orin.

Just as your recovery had reached a point when you could go most of the day with no headache, the time that was spent along Mexico's gulf was cut short by weather. It had happened that as you had left for Florida a hurricane had crossed the northern Mexican peninsula of Yucatan. Once fed with the warmer waters of the Gulf the storm's vortex only strengthened and soon was spinning through the water eastward, back toward Florida. You made haste as was possible, and always you could see the gray edge of the solid cloud to the west as you turned southward. You had heard of the unpredictability of the hurricanes in the Gulf of Mexico and how they had been known to track backwards in their path, seemingly of their own free will. The wind was against you and for a day you knew not if you could out-distance the storm. As it was it took every one of your crew to assist you throughout a day and night to keep the sails in place, and then to bring them down when the gales became too threatening.

Then, early on the third morning you cleared the Gulf and its influences upon your ship. As is often the case the air seemed scrubbed by the passing storm and the clear skies gave favorable winds to your ship's sails. You decided to take advantage of this and the fact that your ship was fully provisioned and you headed south, to the West Indies. You had purchased charts that were mapped as far as Barbados, but could find none that showed any detail of the islands that you knew must lay to the west of the that British possession. Perhaps, you thought, now would be the time to make such charts.

Talia was genuinely thrilled with the idea as she always was. She had never strayed from her declaration that she wanted only to share in that which you wanted to discover. You were her captain, and she was your crew. She loved being busy and the two native boys only added to her enjoyment of planning out her time. She reserved morning and evening to be near you, whether she was helping you to sharpen quills for your map-making, or quietly darning your clothing, her precious sewing box nearby. Her reasoning was that it was imperative, or so she insisted, that you both be available for each other. Soon it was a routine that you both would save certain projects just for these times; knowing that the boys would know not to disturb you. One of these was your wish to draw the more peaceful images of the Starpeople dream you had experienced. You were much better at drawing faces, while Talia excelled at landscapes and water, and clouds. You would spend hours together, usually on the bridge, and while you would describe in fine detail the ships and clothing of the Starpeople, she would draw them in charcoal. Conversely, one of Talia's greatest enjoyments was music. Though neither of you was any good at playing instruments, Talia loved to sing and did so often. Her memory was as impressive as her beauty and she often only had to hear a song once in order to memorize it. One aspect of this that never ceased to make you smile was that most of the songs she had heard were from ports of the Caribbean; songs of drunkenness, wantonness, and general debauchery. The only thing that you insisted upon was that she understood all that she was singing about. She would come to you, fresh from a visit to some port with lyrics ready for your interpretation. Still, she loved the songs, though some she sang only in your presence, and while alone in your cabin.

As for the two brothers, Nine and Seven, you found that Talia seemed to have an instinct on how to approach them. They clearly trusted her completely and they learned English quickly; just to please her you were secretly certain. As for you, so impressed had they been by your fight with the giant Dutchman who had mistreated them that they would often fall still in your presence, watching you. Once, when you had your sword upon your knee while inspecting the edge for imperfections, you were surprised to find the younger of the two boys, Seven, staring at you from a distance. Again he had that look of being almost hypnotized by your movements. Seeing neither Talia nor Nine about you called the boy over to you and asked him if he liked the sword. When he nodded you told him that some day he too could have a sword like the one you held. He seemed to think about it and even closed his eyes for a moment, as though it would help him to consider. Again looking at you he asked, "Could I have this one?"

You could see the youngster was serious, very serious in fact, and you fought not to smile. "There are many swords, Seven. Many are much finer than mine. Why do you want this one?"

He reached out a small hand as though to touch it, and then drew back. "Because it is yours," he told you, and when he saw your puzzled expression he added, "it is the one that you used that stopped the giant from killing me and my brother."

"Yes, but this is the ship that rescued you from the giant. Do you want it also?"

Without hesitation the boy stated, "I do."

The ship, you told Seven, belonged to Talia since the gold and everything it bought was hers. As for the sword, you had won it gambling, so you had assured Seven that when you were done with the blade, he could have it. Then, with the same serious tone as the child you added, "Keep in mind Seven, if I die fighting, you may have to wait a very long time to get this sword."

The child did not see the humor and in fact Seven had agreed with all seriousness that he would wait until you were completely finished with the sword.

You were aware of the effect you had on the boys, but this incident drove home just how much of an effect you had. You had left all aspects of their education up to Talia, who flourished under the task, and they even called her 'mother', but now you decided that you would take a little more time with them, especially this younger one who was so serious all of the time. When you made your forays into a new port, whether for supplies or simply to see the lay of the land and the cut of the people, it became your habit to take Seven with you, and quickly you grew accustomed to his presence as he helped with duties, and stayed as silent as a stone during your transactions. To most people he appeared as a slave, but you had no fear that you were mistreating the child. Each time you returned to the ship he would joyously run to his brother and relate, not the sights and sounds he had just witnessed, but the sort of things he had been allowed to do to help you, such as to carry the newly purchased basket of bread, or to hold your tri-cornered hat as you passed through a tavern.

As for Seven's older brother Nine, the boy seemed dedicated to Talia. While at first he was noticeably protective of his brother, he soon relaxed under Talia's care, though he insisted as long as you knew him that he had to sleep with his brother, in the same bed. Seven would sometimes wake screaming with nightmares and only Nine's presence would help to calm him. When the seven year old grew older, the screaming stopped, but not the dreams, and so Nine remained with his brother.

You were surprised how easily Talia and Nine spoke to each other, and on any subject. Though he was quiet by nature, he was not the dark serious youth Seven was. He laughed easily and would go to great lengths to make Talia smile, such as one day climbing a tree to bring her a piece of fruit she desired. The season was late and the locals had all but stripped the tree of its bounty; a fact Talia had lamented. She had mentioned how she wished she could jump high enough to reach the elusive piece of fruit she had spotted, a good fifty feet above. Before Talia realized what he was doing Nine was half way up the tree with Seven at the bottom cheering him on. It was then that you had found out that the child had been trained to climb trees, and when asked he explained that he had been taught to hunt birds for food and their feathers. To his people, he explained, feathers were as good as currency. When asked, he happily explained how he used a dart gun; blowing small darts made from bones and feathers of birds through a hollow reed, which had been hardened with resin. The goal was not to immediately kill the bird, but stun it enough to bring it down. If the feather were good some would be removed, but only ones not critical to the bird for flight. Then it would be released, so that it could grow more and provide feathers at a later time. If the bird was good for food, it was then dispatched and carried home.

He had been relating this to both of you, with Seven listening while you were all on the deck of the Angel Orin. Privately, you and Talia had decided to not ask the boys about their past and let them discuss it as they wished. Seven never did so, but every now and then, usually when you and Seven were on land Nine would tell Talia about their journey to the ocean. He had never seen the ocean before and Talia noticed that he used it like a metaphor; his reaching the ocean clearly marked a change for him, for his reality. There were two; another was the white stone. As far as Talia could make out there was time "Before the white stone" and a time "Before the ocean". He would say things like, "We used to go to school before the white stone," or "We met the man in the black robe before the ocean."

"They seemed to have walked for a long time." Talia told you one evening. "Maybe even a year."

This impressed you. "A year? Those two children?"

Talia agreed that it sounded fantastic. "Nine mentioned that they would get presents of food and messages from some sort of nature god as to where they should turn, so I think they had some help."

You agreed it was mysterious. You had shown them the golden jewelry and beads and while it was clear that they had not seen gold metal before, they were familiar with each of the animals, including the crocodile standing on his hands. Talia had asked the boys if they knew why the reptile was in such a strange position, and Nine admitted that he did not know. When Seven did not reply, Talia thought he had not heard and asked her question again. To her surprise Seven narrowed his eyes suspiciously and told her, almost commanding, "You cannot ask that question."

You reminded the younger boy that you tolerated no disrespect to Talia yet Seven only repeated his command, even louder in his apparent distress, "She cannot ask that question!"

As you put down the charcoal that you had been crushing for ink and stood ready to face the child, you were stopped when Nine suddenly ran across the galley where you had gathered and tackled the younger boy to the hard wood flooring. Before

Seven could rise, Nine was already on his feet
pleading with you to forgive his brother. The act
subdued Seven completely and he stayed on the floor,
covering his eyes with his hands. It was clear that this
was not the first time that Seven had behaved in this
emotionally charged manner, nor was it the first time
that Nine had defended him in this unusual fashion
because of it. You could only imagine the trouble
such behavior would cause in a slave, and your
opinion of Nine grew. You and Talia had both thought
it best to let the matter fall away, to Nine's obvious
relief. Later the older boy would confide in Talia that
the incident of the crocodile bead was one that touch
his brother's religious nature. He told her that once
his brother became upset concerning something
having to do with religion, it was impossible to stop
him without drastic measures, such as what you had
witnessed in the galley. You both wondered at how
such a young child could be so deeply involved in
such a complicated subject as religion. Nine insisted
that he could say no more about it, except to admit
that he did not discuss religion with his brother, ever.

It was easy enough to avoid discussing
religion; it was not a subject you or Talia cared for,
but you did want the children to know about the
Starpeople, if only for Talia's sake. Those heavenly
people came up often in conversation, especially at
night with a clear sky full of stars, and you did not
want the name of the Starpeople disparaged in front
of Talia. But there was nothing to fear. You and her

were both pleased to find that both children knew stories from their origins of people who sounded the same, though they sailed canoes instead of the gilded three masted ships you had seen.

The months became a year, and the year became two as your crew settled into a well formed pattern. Each person enjoyed their duties upon the ship and land; Talia was very fond of routine and you and the boys had no trouble with this. It kept not only the ship in wonderful shape, but the three of you as well.

Creating charts from blank pieces of parchment took painstaking focus, of which you had plenty, but it also took patience on your part, of which you had little, and you thrived on the daily challenge. The islands that rested in waters of the West Indies had more than a life-time's mystery waiting to be explored. The frequent storms that assailed areas like Florida and Mexico were not so common here, and people had been able to build sizable social centers, such as on Barbados. So populous was this place that you found yourself there often for supplies, since that is where most merchants purchased their own stock, only to mark it up tenfold in their own shops. Owned by the British, the island had its own Assay officers who weighed and bought gold and silver for the government. Practically surrounded by unfriendly countries, these officers, thousands of miles from England, did not ask questions as to the source of the precious metals they purchased - it was assumed the Spaniards were involved. It was to these that you had taken much of the jewelry.

The average officer that worked on Barbados was clearly being punished for some misdeed he had done in England, or so each would have you believe as you dealt with them. There were many places to exchange gold about the island, most in the congested port of Bridgetown. They were sometimes set up on the docks for the ships coming in, but all were unhappy. Seeing you for a countryman, they would immediately ask for news of home but once they knew you were captain of a ship they fairly ignored your presence. Never did you notice one take an interest in the make or model of the jewelry. Each would simply drop your gold, in what ever form, onto the scale and weigh it out. Once he transferred it to silver the gold was unceremoniously dumped into the iron box with the rest of the day's take of gold and locked up.

It was to one of these Assay officers in Bridgetown you were going when you spotted the flag of the Ottawa Fleet. The island was a producer of cotton and rum; there was no reason for traders of fur and cold water fish to be in these parts. Taking the ship to a more hidden location, you decided that you had to find out what this ship was doing here.

Knowing the anxiety it would cause Talia, you confided in the boys and with the night to cover your face as well as your movements you went to town.

Waiting until after midnight, you watched as the Ottawa crew grew drunk, and picked out one sailor who liked to talk. You bought him a few rounds under the same pretense as the British officers; you wanted news from England. Since he had not been back to that country in years, but he wanted the ale, he was more than willing to tell you tales of his adventures along the eastern Atlantic seaboard and the frozen northern lands. Most of the sailor's stories were truthful, you knew since having been there, only his experiences were inflated to that instead of a six foot bear, his fight involved one that was twenty feet tall. But you pretended to believe every word, and after praising his extreme prowess against nature, asked him what could have ever drawn him to such peaceful waters as the West Indies.

It took everything for you to keep a calm stance when your name was immediately mentioned. The sailor was drunk enough that he was willing to complain about his lot, and how slighted he had felt at being sent on a "wild goose chase" after some rogue who had stolen his bosses' wife.

"Cuckolded he was, and so he stayed, if you ask me." the drunk man had insisted, spitting on the floor to punctuate his disgust. "Been searchin' for years, and caught up to him twice, but didn't do any good. Lost the rogue each time! "Then he took another swig and shrugged, "But whom I am to complain, the bloody judge? It's a livin'."

It was then that you asked how he kept finding the "rogue" and the sailor's answer was like a strike of thunder to you - the gold jewelry.

The Spaniards were still very busy with their conquest of Mexico and while most of the land along the coasts had been subjugated generations before, they had barely touched the interior. This was especially true of the southern lands where the thick jungle acted like a living wall to the bulky trappings of the Europeans and their horses. A few times each year there would be word of a village, or circuit of villages that had not yet fallen under the capable hands of the Spaniards, and soon new slaves and goods would suddenly flood the market. So had this very thing happened a few years before you had found that small treasure chest. The entire collection had been much larger, and many of the common soldiers had stolen jewelry in their first murderous raids against the homes of the villagers. These escaped the legal transfer to the Spanish Viceroy and therefore the hands of the Spanish crown and slipped directly into the currency of the markets.

That had been years ago and the jewelry had fallen out of use as it was melted down or sold to foreign lands far away. For it to suddenly show up again had caused some talk which somehow had gotten to Young. He probably knew about the connection before in the Caribbean when he bombed his own ship and had thought to kill you there. The drunken sailor explained how the harbor master had told everyone that if they saw the strange jewelry in their travels, to report it to him for a reward. Someone had and now Wallace Young had traced the jewelry to Barbados, and to you.

Without hesitation you took the ship away from Barbados, effectively loosing Angel Orin among the islands to the west. It bothered you that the supplies you had hoped to purchase were left behind, but for the moment you could see no hope for it. The basics of food and water could be found along the smaller villages but ultimately you wanted to go even further south. If you were careful perhaps you could look for the unexplored islands thought to be to the south long enough for Young to lose interest in your trail. To do that would require extensive provisioning which you did not have.

You struggled with whether you should share this news with Talia or not. Her amazing capacity for happiness astounded you and every day she found new reasons to validate that happiness. For instance, she recently discovered how to press flowers and leaves and such in tremendous books formed for that purpose. Chemically treated paper preserved her specimens and it gave her yet another of her enjoyable "tasks' whenever you made landfall. The thought of causing a disruption to her blossoming life was almost painful to you. She had been so cheated as a child that it did not seem fair to you to take away her happiness now, only to replace it with distress and worries which may never come to pass. So you withheld your newly acquired knowledge of the Ottawa fleet from her. But there was one thing you did share with her, though she did not know your real reason for doing so. You had some gold left in the form of Spanish coins and these you asked Talia to sew these into the lining of the bag that she always carried when upon land. You told her truthfully that they were for her to use whenever she felt the need.

Soon you were as prepared as you could be with the supplies you had been able to secure from the smaller communities to the west. One morning before sunrise you stood alone on the deck, again going over the list of provisions in your head. You had not slept well. Your dreams were disturbed by scenes of giant ocean waves, threatening to overturn Angel Orin and her crew. From your vantage point overhead you could only watch, knowing that what you witnessed had to be. You woke in a sweat, knowing that the ship would not escape the towering waves in the dream.

You knew your disturbed sleep was from stress. You wanted to head south but you did not think you had what you would need to successfully ply those open waters and return with the favorable winds before your supplies ran out. And then there was the matter of the gold. You did not want to spend the coins that were left; that was Talia's insurance should anything happen to you, and you would rather return to gambling, you decided, than take that from her.

And then an idea came to you; you could gamble the gold jewelry. If you were to lose a bead or two in a bet, then the next hand would be pressed coin and you could win that. A dark enough tavern, and a drunken enough crowd and no one would care what the gold looked like as long as it was gold. But you would have to do it quickly and that meant that you had to go somewhere with many taverns, where you could play many different games. Cards, dice, darts, whatever they had, you were prepared to try it, betting one bead at a time. You figured if you played for two, maybe three nights like that, you should be able to get the gold and silver coin you needed and leave before the beads could be traced back to you. The only flaw to the plan was that the only place big enough to hold that many gamblers was Barbados.

This plan you confided in with Nine and Seven, mainly because you needed their help to pull it off. Both were wary knowing that one of Young's ships had just been seen in the area, but mostly because you asked them to lie to Talia. You told her that the ship needed supplies from Barbados one more time before your great journey south, and after she had fallen asleep, you would quietly make your way to town, Seven in tow.

Things went well enough the first night. With Seven as your eyes, he kept watch for any ship with the Ottawa flag, and seeing none, you wondered if the ship had returned north. The second night was just as the first and you knew the success of it lay in the fact that you did not stay too long at any one game or one tavern. Upon retiring the second night you considered if you had enough pressed coin in your possession. What troubled your sleep yet another night was the fact that concerning your plan to go south, you were headed toward uncharted waters. Not knowing what to expect, you did not know how to plan accordingly. Never would you have thought to begin such a journey as this at such a sudden and unprepared time; but you did not know in what other direction to go in order to save Talia from Wallace Young. Watching the sun rise upon the third morning, you decided that you would go to the taverns one more time.

Bridgetown was never fully dark. Torches and cooking fires burned everywhere, keeping the flying insects away and casting the place in a perpetual orange glow at night. But there were also shadows, especially along the waterfront where the taverns lay and to these did you and Seven keep. Again you had both had spent hours before even entering the town looking for signs of the Ottawan flag and though you had spotted none, that did not stop you from keeping your guard up. The harbor was large with miles of coast and there were close to one hundred taverns strung along its edge. You decided to stay toward the southern end; there would you be closer to where you had left Angel Orin, anchored offshore with Nine manning the decks while Talia slept.

The night had been proceeding well. The

taverns were crowded with sailors and almost every table had some game going on. So far no one had remarked upon the strange designs of the beads you were betting, and you were beginning to think that you might have won enough in gold and silver coin to satisfy you. This decision came about at near three o'clock in the morning while you gambled in a tavern called The Rusty Axe. It was housed in a large wooden building with no windows, but small slits cut throughout the planks to allow light in the daytime and helped to capture any breeze that might me passing by. It's full second floor told you it was also a brothel. The Rusty Axe's fine carved sign was a colorful play on the sounds of words; a large red rooster carrying an axe under its right wing. By this you knew the place was owned by a Scotsman.

It was clearly a popular place and many people were willing to stand while they had their ale or made inquiries as to the price of the ladies of the house. You had not been here long, perhaps enough to roll three casts of the dice and play one hand of Dead Jack Spade. This hand you had lost, and you were planning your departure of Bridgetown upon the next deal of the cards, which you planned to win.

As hard as he had tried not to, Seven had fallen asleep and you had pushed him under your bench where he would not be stepped on. You had been aware of this from the moment he had nodded off, and had been watching the tavern's three doors for any face you might recognize Now that you had

decided to leave soon, you woke and bid Seven to
stand ready to go. Winning the hand with a touch of
mock surprise, you had just cinched the knot on your
money bag when something familiar caught your eye
at one of the tavern's doors. Your body seemed to
realize what it was before your eyes had the chance to
focus as your heart began to race, seemingly of its
own accord and just before you turned to look at that
doorway you knew it was Wallace Young. Facing him
you could see that he was smiling and gazing directly
at you. His eyes were narrowed and you knew that he
had every intention of killing you.

With the shadows of the long table hiding your
movements you passed the money bag to Seven,
never taking your eyes from Young. Then, in a low
tone that brooked no argument, you told the boy in a
whisper,

"Go back to the ship."

As Seven made his escape you could tell by
Young's unflinching gaze that the harbor master had
not seen the young boy's movements. Giving the
child a few moments to clear the area you returned
the older man's smile with one of your own, and
while Young's face was murderous, your expression
was one of satisfaction. This had the effect you were
looking for as Young's smirk turned into a grimace of
hatred and the rotund man straightened with
indignation in the doorway. Seeing the harbor
master's new agitation as it clearly unsettled the man,
you made your move. You had known the location of

each of the four doors of the tavern before you had even entered the Rusty Axe and now you bolted to the one closest to you. From Young's earlier smile you assumed he had men with him nearby, but as you left the building you realized that he had brought many more than just a simple ship's crew. It took you only a moment to see that the tavern was surrounded. You knew the harbor master would never have been granted this amount of force in the name of the company to search for you in the West Indies. You wondered how much it had cost the Young to hire this small army. The older man had been wealthy when you had met him in the far north, but no harbor master earned enough to support such a quest as Wallace Young had set against you and Talia for these many years.

Certainly this last attempt had cost the man dearly, and he had traded practically all he had owned for this last venture south. Young had sold his shares of the company, becoming in effect a servant of the Ottowa fleet, and perhaps even more telling the obsessed man had traded his ship to the small force he had hired to find and destroy you. "If you end this for me, " he had told them in the colonies of New Amsterdam, "you will own the vessel that carries you." Upon hearing the conditions of their employment the hired men wondered if perhaps their employer was not sane; a ship for the capture of one man, for that had been the agreement, seemed crazy, even for a man consumed with jealously. Young had spent much time impressing upon them that the man in question was not to be killed outright: he was to be tried by the harbor master himself and then hanged as a pirate upon the land where he was found. The dead man's possessions were to be given to the harbor master himself, including the woman known to travel with the pirate. Young did not tell them that Talia was his wife, though there were those among the crew who knew the fact, and secretly shared it with the mercenaries.

A feeling of impeding doom came upon you as your realized your predicament, but it was not, by far, the strongest feeling within you. Instead of fear, or even concern for what must certainly happen next, your strongest emotion was anger. This anger was not just the familiar disappointment you had always felt in the human race for its weaknesses and foibles. Neither was it the smoldering hatred you felt for Wallace Young's unrelenting torture of Talia, whether when he was hounding her steps or haunting her dreams as nightmares with her memories of his abuse. Your emotion now was deeper than that, for it encompassed the world. You knew you would not escape this day and that you would die in this place. Truly that did not bother you, for you had every faith that you would be meeting the very Starpeople who had been introduced to in your fever dreams. But you could not pretend to abide the fact that you would be leaving Talia to continue without you, and the sadness it would cause her. Your anger stemmed from the sheer unfairness of it and with a passion you had not known before, you decided that you would do the one thing for Talia left in your power to do; you would rid her of the man who had worked so hard to ruin her life. You would kill Wallace Young.

All of this had been contemplated and decided upon within the span of a heartbeat and with the next you turned back into the building. Wallace still stood in the doorway, though he had entered a few paces to pursue you with another man just behind him. Seeing your purpose in your eyes even as you drew your sword, the man ran back outside but Young had no time to react. As the large man fell backwards his shocked expression told you that he knew without doubt that you had won. Your sword pierced him exactly where you had aimed, straight into his heart, and your force behind the move sent you falling to the side as well and plunging the sword to its hilt. He died instantly. You barely noticed the rough hands of Young's hired mob as they grabbed you and you peered at the older man's face looking for signs of life. Satisfied that you saw none, your thoughts were taken over by the knowledge that Talia was now truly free of this monster that had so dominated her life. You knew you were being taken out into the night air, but it did not seem to concern you. There was nothing any one could do that would change that fact that Talia was now free. You felt a heavy rope as it was placed around your neck, and somewhere in your mind you knew it was meant to be the means that would end your life, but it only served to remind you of Talia's necklace of golden bees that she cherished so well. In your mind you could see again how the light of the sun reflected little sparkles of radiance against her skin when she wore it on a clear day. The captain of the Starpeople had recognized that necklace and the memory of that dream turned your thoughts to them. Looking upward toward the stars, the image of their lofty golden sails came to mind, and you could picture them against the bright stars that covered the night sky.

You thought someone asked you if you had any last words, and you fought for a moment to understand what he meant. Certainly any thing you had to say would be said to Talia, and never would your love for her allow a word to be the "last" between you. But then you realized that you did have a message you wished to give to Talia, and you glanced around for Seven. A large crowd had gathered at the commotion, and you could see the boy safely hidden among them, silently watching. Turning your attention back to the glittering sky you announced loudly, seemingly to no one,

"Tell her I will be a captain of the Starpeople, and to look for my ship."

The crowd that had assembled outside had not been disappointed at the sudden intrusion upon their nocturnal debaucheries. They were impressed by this young man who had warranted such a force as the small army that stood before them now. The dashing young man had killed their captain with one blow and now the rascal smiled, seemingly at the sky, as he was being hanged for it. It was as though he had won after all and did not care that he was soon to die. Regardless of the crimes this man might have been accused of, all the people present - Young's men included - agreed that he was dying both bravely and honorably. If anything the man looked satisfied, as though he had accomplished all he could have hoped and did not rue that his time was done. He stood as straight as a captain upon the brow of his ship, confident in the course he had set. This only served to add to their admiration of him.

As for Westly, he knew he would have to keep his promise to Talia that he would return to her with the Starpeople. He had smiled when he saw Seven's small form running back in the direction of the ship, knowing that his message would be delivered, Turning his attention to his next task, he did not notice when he was led to a tall, thin tree and hoisted onto one of the tavern's wooden stools. Instead he was thinking of the Starpeople. It seemed that they should be able to hear him; if not his words then at least his feelings and his intentions. There was no doubt within him; he fully intended to join those travelers in the sky, and he cast that thought upward to the stars. He knew there had been no time in his life when he would have been called "religious", nor was he now. But he did believe that there was more to the universe besides the doings of one little planet, and forces greater than what was known to mankind. It was to this greatness that Westly directed his wish, and his intention to continue to be a part of Talia's life through the Starpeople.

He noticed that his heart was slowing, and he realized that he did not have much time. He could no longer see or feel anything, but it did not bother him, since he needed none of those faculties to continue with his plan. He brought to his mind every memory he had of the Starpeople, his dreams as well as the many conversations with Talia concerning them. He wanted to make certain that his last thought upon Earth would be about them, and his wish to return to Talia. With his last heartbeat he commended his life, his death, and all that it had meant to his love for Talia. She represented all about human beings that was beautiful and trusting and kind; all things Westly had decided did not exist before knowing her. She had not only given the young man's life purpose, she had given it soul. Sent before him as a beacon to light his way, he prayed, "For Talia, young as a sunrise yet just as alone as when it sets; without tear, without regret, a promise I shall never forget..'

Westly did not realized just how silent the world had become until he heard someone call his name. Just a moment before his pulse had been like thunder in his ears and he decided that his heart must have finally stopped.

He was not surprised to find that the transition from life to death seemed to feel so natural to him, for Westly had seen plenty of men die in his short life. The idea had never bothered him as it did many people, and even now he felt no horror or repulsion at his new situation. Instead he felt the same familiar drive to be with Talia that he had experienced since the day he had met her. After the initial realization that his heart had stopped and he was indeed dead, he had turned his thoughts to the voice that he had heard. Among the darkness that surrounded his senses, he asked within his mind who it was that had called to him by name. Listening for the answer Westly was startled when the masculine voice replied with its own question:

"Where is Talia?"

When Talia woke the next morning, she knew you had not returned to her bed and she rose in a flurry knowing you had come to harm. She ran to the deck to find Nine and Seven sitting on the wooden flooring. They had obviously been there for hours, facing the hatchway that led to the captain's berth, and waiting for her to awaken. Nine's eyes were red from crying and he had an arm protectively encircling Seven. As for the younger brother, he sat motionless, his eyes cast downward. The young woman quietly lowered herself to the deck next to them and trying to control her voice, managed to whispered, "Seven, what has happened to Westly?"

At the sound of her voice the boy looked up at her. While his face was expressionless, his eyes were narrowed in anger and Talia recognized that look; Seven was angry with his gods. Upon seeing the young woman before him his eyes widened and he began to shake. He had literally lost his mother when he was five years old, and Talia had filled that role admirably when he had needed it the most. He would have done anything for her; even die if that would have helped her. And now she was asking him something he would never wish to give her; an explanation of what happened to her husband, the joy of her life, and her one great love. He watched in a daze of appalling horror as her pained expression grew while she tried in vain to wait patiently for his answer. It was clear that she knew her husband was dead, and softly, almost in a whisper, she prodded the boy, asking simply, "How?"

As gently as she had tried to ask the question, it was as a physical blow to Seven. The child shook his head; it was all that he could do. He would open his mouth, but nothing would come out. It was like the answer to her simple question of what had happened to Westly was too big for him to give. Finally, not knowing what do to, his covered his eyes with his hands.

Nine nodded knowingly, and held his brother closer. Then, placing his free hand upon Talia's shoulder, the older boy explained the sequence of events as Seven had told him earlier. Just as he came to Westly's final words, his brother suddenly reached up and stopped him by placing a small hand over Nine's mouth.

"He told me to tell her!" the younger boy declared with renewed fortitude. Jumping to his feet, he looked down at her and handed over the bag of pressed European coin that Westly had won. Then he told her in a voice strained by grief, "Captain Westly Shane has returned to the Starpeople to become a captain, and he has instructed you to look for his ship. "

When Seven was done Talia closed her eyes, recreating the scene in her mind, and Westly as he spoke his final words. She was stunned, it was true, and she wondered how it was that she did not simply die at the news of Westly's demise. But foremost in her mind was his promise. If she were to break down now it would seem like an affront to all that Westly had stood for. He had always been a man of action; if you did not like something you did something about it. Even in death Westly had taken control of the situation. By killing the vicious Wallace Young he had freed her forever. Westly had even thought to send the money back with Seven in the midst of his danger. But when most men would be pleading for their lives, Westly was still working, this time charting the unknown waters that led to the Starpeople. Talia had no doubt that Westly would succeed in all that he had said, and looking up into the tropical skies she imagined the day when she would see Westly dressed as the captain of a starship, just as he had described the great ships of the Starpeople to her. He would keep his promise, she had no doubt. Allowing herself a sigh in which to voice her sadness, she too made a promise. She swore that she would never forget to watch for his return. Then, she swore aloud to no one; "I will be there."

Again you closed your eyes. After the all-encompassing darkness that had marked the end of your heart's beating, the sun in the sky seemed even brighter than usual. Your body was as confused as you were; you knew you were supposed to be dead, yet you could surely feel the breeze upon your skin, and even felt that you could taste the salt of the ocean spray upon your lips. Then you heard the voices that had been lingering on the edge of your perception, and you realized that they were telling you the details of your demise. Their voices both gentle and yet insistent; it seemed important to them that you understand what they were saying. Three times they described the event, each time asking you if you remembered. But as hard as your tried you could recall clearly only your promise to Talia, that you would find the Starpeople and return to her. Then, upon contemplating that promise, in a sudden flash you knew you had succeeded. You were with the Starpeople. They had come for you, and while you were forced to leave your body behind on the island of Barbados, the Starpeople's crew had retrieved your soul. Now you understood what the voices had been explaining to you. You heard the man who had first called your name as he explained to you that as far as the Starpeople were concerned there was little difference between the states of being alive and being dead. Both processes were natural and as common as a breath going in, followed by the same breath going out. You nodded your understanding and heard the man say,

"I am glad to see that you are beginning to comprehend, Westly. We have much work to do." Then he asked, "Where is Talia?"

His question was like a powerful elixir. You felt an energy run through you, and a feeling of strength entered your limbs. In all of this recent confusion Talia had remained the one constant; nothing made sense without her. Everything you had done, and were doing now was for her. And you had succeeded. You had rescued her from Wallace Young, and had taught her how to survive on her own. "Alive!" you declared your answer to his question and added, "She now captains Angel Orin." You pictured her on the deck of that fine ship, her long hair streaming in the breeze. "She is underway." you noticed aloud.

She was always happy in her form no matter what she was doing, and you were startled to see that in your memory of her now, she was not. Instead, her shoulders were slumped and she was gazing sadly at the distant horizon where the ship was headed. Never had you seen her so sad, and you knew it was because of you.

Before you knew it, your eyes were opened and you were sitting up on a bunk in the hull of a great ship. Sitting in a chair next to you was the captain you had seen in your dreams, his expression both somber and kind.

"How will we find her?" you asked and realized it had sounded like a command. But the man did not seem to notice and answered,

"The same way in which we found you."

The man bid you to follow him, and you found yourself crossing the deck of the ship to the helm. A crew worked busily about you, but your attention was taken by the sea and the sky, which were not like any you had ever seen, even in the strangest of ocean storms.

The ship was in motion, her silken golden sails full with a breeze that seemed to come from the stars themselves. The huge vessel seemed to be gliding on a thin sea of silver light that stretched as far as you could see in all directions. The thickness of a ship's plank, the sea shimmered with energy as you passed through it, causing sparkling waves of silver in the ship's wake. The unusual sea was almost transparent and you could see an array of stars and galaxies in the sky both above and below. The colors of the myriad of stars were astounding, and the range of those colors surpassed any you had seen, even upon the flowers of the tropical islands. Everything seemed close, and you could even see the details of the surface of the moon as it hung above you. Glancing over the edge of the ship's gilded railing, you were stunned to see the very Earth below you. It was approaching night but its blue oceans clearly dominated the view. From your time spent charting and creating maps, you could tell that you were over the West Indies, although the islands appeared as specks from this vantage point. Though you knew you could not see it, you looked to where you thought Angel Orin might be, carrying Talia and the two brothers with her.

"You will be the navigator." You heard the captain tell you.

Gesturing to that immense blue ocean below you asked, "How?"

You knew much about ships and their navigation, but you could not see how anyone could master such a great ship as this one through these incredible forces of nature. Certainly the experienced captain of the Starpeople, you thought, but a mere mortal such as yourself?

The captain led you from the view below and back to the ship's helm. Like the rest of the ship, it was of the finest make, and adorned with accents of brass. Made in the shape of a compass, it had an inner wheel that looked more like a clock than a steering mechanism.

"You wish to go to your Talia," he told you.

"So think of her - think of her as she thinks of you. Did you not tell her to look for you?" The captain then bid you to put your hands upon the wheel.

You imagined her quietly watching the stars from the deck of the ship, and a part of you knew without doubt that she would do this. When you had this picture in your mind firmly the dark starry night began to lighten. Willing yourself, you concentrated upon her face looking upward. The ship went to where your emotions lead, to home.

You passed between two great white clouds and could see the ship below, the sails open and cutting swiftly through the waves. Talia was there as you imagined her, facing upward, but toward the crow's nest. Nine was calling to her, pointing behind. So taken you were to see Talia again you had to pull your attention from her forcefully to see where Nine indicated.

A three masted Spanish galleon closing in quickly. You had run into such ships before in the Mediterranean and knew your old ship was no match for long. You quickly asked the captain how many cannons the ship carried.

"None."

You asked how he defended his crew.

"By avoiding offense," was the only reply. You wanted to argue-accuse him of lying, but his face told you he was sincere. You frantically thought what else you might do, then said to put you on your own ship, so that you might help defend.

"You have not an earthly body," they reminded you.

Again you struggled to form a plan, looking upon the ships below, as they grew ever nearer. Almost shouting you told the captain to bring his ship between the two racing below.

"You are the navigator. The one who can do this is you alone".

'Then show me how." you insisted.

"We have."

You tried to imagine the ship moving downward between them but the Star People's ship only hovered about Talia.

"You must be able to hold the image," the captain told you.

"There is no time!" you replied.

"Do not consider the time then, consider only the moment," he told you. You thought of the moment, forcing yourself to keep your focus upon the horribly large galleon bearing down upon the ship that carried your only family-soon to be in cannon range. So large those Spanish sails they caught the winds like a wall of a cathedral. To move between them quickly enough you would need a gale wind to fill the yellow sails and drive the Star People's ship toward the galleon.

Suddenly you felt the ship move from its stillness, the sails snapped taunt from an unseen wind, and you headed toward the galleon. So swift was the distance crossed you thought you were going to ram the Spanish.

But just as you readied yourself for the impact, the ship stopped, and the wind died not only from your sails but also the sails of the galleon. As for Talia, her ship continued at its top speed, quickly gaining a fair distance.

You could see the faces of the Spaniards filled with terror. "Diablo-devils!" they exclaimed, crossing their hearts and some falling to their knees in prayer.

"You are the only devils here!" you shouted, but you could tell they could not see you or the Star People's ship. "How can they not see us when we made their vessel stop?" you asked.

"We did not stop them, the wind did. You asked for the calmness by wishing for a gale. Your true desire that moment was to stop this powerful ship from catching Talia. Your idea to achieve this was the gale, but earth's winds had a different idea, since they better know their own nature. The wind stopped carrying the galleon and continued to carry Talia."

"How long will the wind refuse to carry them?" you asked.

"Until they can no longer catch Talia."

When at last the wind returned you asked if the captain had a destination.

"Certainly," they told you. "Where nothing is measured. A journey for its own sake. We change our course and direction by the rise and fall of tides of emotion."

"But you must have a final destination," you

insisted.

"As long as there is one creature who will wonder if there are people from the stars, our ship will fly. A different crew perhaps but always there."

When you heard this you said you wished to be with Talia-not a crew member of the ship.

She had discoveries yet to make upon earth, they told you, but when she finished you would be together.

You knew they spoke truly~she was still alive, but you did not know how you would be able to wait for her. You asked the captain's leave to take the ship to Talia and, consenting, you had no trouble finding her. The ship was far out to sea and still with sails full. You knew what Talia was planning-get out of range of all spy scopes and wait till supplies forced a return. That had been your plan. Talia had always been a fast learner.

The three of them were kept busy with the rigging and steering. As you followed above them you asked how you might make Talia hear you.

"We can make nothing here, it is not our place to do so."

"Then how did I see you?" you asked.

"Because you were looking. Even at your earthly end you thought of us-that is what led us to you. When Talia looks for you-you will know."

"Then I will wait until she does." You told the captain you would wait a hundred years if needed.

"That is admirable," the captain replied, then

added, "Do not forget Westly, consider only the moment and consider not the time."

You continued to watch Talia as she now looked at your old navigational charts. The boys ran about taking care of this and that.

'They are very busy at this moment," the captain remarked.

"Yes," you agreed, then told him, "They learned how to run a ship when I was wounded and could not."

"They run it well," he agreed, then asked when you thought they might weigh anchor.

"Not till nightfall."

"Then let us return at that moment," he suggested.

You did not want to leave her, not even for one instant, but you knew the wisdom within the captain's words. Talia would not have the luxury to look among the stars until the ship and gear was secured and with only the three of them it would be hard.

"Can I take us to the moment I wished?" you asked. The captain nodded. "Any moment you wish Westly, as long as you can imagine it in your mind with no doubt of the possibility of the image."

You thought of the ship at rest and Talia coming above to walk the deck after their dinner. But scene below remained and you asked the captain why.

"They are very brave, and they work very hard," he told you, then added, "You especially know how much effort they spend since you too have worked so hard with them. You were proud of work, Westly, were you not?"

" Of course," you told him.

"And are you not proud of their hard efforts at this moment?" he answered for you, "Of course you are-and so are we. It is because of this that our ship does not carry you further. You wish them to have their moments of work as well as rest. Let them have their chores-we will return when they have finished. In the meantime we can harbor at another place."

"Where?" you asked.

"Any place or moment we wish to be Westly," he told you.

"Where do you wish to be?" you asked.

"I welcome new ports in which to discover new understanding, but naturally, I too have my chosen ports of call."

"Where do you consider home?" you asked.

"My home is this ship. Some of our crew also feel the same, but some are here as passengers and they we help to reach their desired destination."

"Am I a passenger?" you asked, but the captain asked in turn,

"Are you a passenger?"

The captain left, suggesting you let yourself time to think but you could only wonder how Talia and the boys were doing on their own. You watched them below as they weighed anchor and after securing sails went below. Night was falling, bringing rain-laden clouds with it. Soon the Star People's ship was surrounded by the storm and the captain approached, soaked by the rain.

He told you smiling, 'This is your chosen place to be at the moment, Westly, but would you mind taking us a bit above these clouds?"

Feeling more than a little foolish you had apologized for the inconvenience and asked the captain to pick the next destination.

He told you, "When you wish to return you need only mention it."

Many places and moments did you experience. Many times did you think of Talia, especially at times when the ship drifted above the oceans of earth. Many were the times you thought of returning but each time, you imagined her busy with the things of daily existence. You could easily recall the look of determination on her face when she was fronted by long odds. She loved the life she had upon the water just as you had, and you knew she would work all the harder to keep it.

So you too stayed busy aboard your new ship, learning how feelings of emotion could steer the vessel and the focus needed to choose one moment from lifetimes of memories. The passengers were many also, though there was no duration of time, which you could measure. One would disembark upon a world circling a blue sun at night, and the next night disembark upon a ball of air in a red web of glittering dew. Whoever chooses the destination was the navigator.

Then there were moments when it could be call drifting, when the ship would be allowed to follow its own course. It was then you learned that the beautiful vessel was itself alive. It seemed to know where it wished to go; always one who had just finished their life on earth, as you had, and like yourself had thought of people among the stars. Then the ship would stay on course until they were found.

It was just after such a voyage when floating above the new arrival's ancestral home in Africa you suddenly thought of Talia. She was not working as you usually imagined, but crying. You rushed to the captain, but he already knew.

"Take the helm Westly," he told you.

You were surprised to find the ship where you had last seen it, far off the coast of the Cayman Isles. The boys were on deck swabbing water from a recent rain.

"Talia must be below," you said.

The captain replied, "Go to her."

"How?" you asked.

"Think of her thinking of you."

You closed your eyes and concentrated, knowing that the captain was speaking true, you could go to her.

You heard Talia call your name, and you opened your eyes to find yourself in your old cabin. It was just as you recalled, though much darker. Talia was sitting at the small table near the porthole, staring at the navigational charts. You softly called her name unsure of what effect or any it would have, she sighed and said aloud,

"Oh Westly, how dearly you are missed," yet her eyes remained upon the worn charts.

"I am sorry," you told her. "I did not wish to leave you so suddenly."

She said softly, "I know you did not want to leave me."

It was then you realized that while she could not see or hear you she could in some way feel you; your presence.

Again she broke into tears, and you thought your own heart would break at the sound of her sobbing. Unthinking you rushed to her side, kneeling you laid your hand upon hers, you could feel its warmth. Talia felt something as well, but what you did not know. She suddenly stopped crying and pulling her hand away, looked at it; puzzled.

"Do not be afraid," you told her.

She again sighed and said looking upward, "I am trying to be strong, Westly. I want to raise Seven and Nine on our boat as we had planned, but I cannot even learn where we are!" Tears came to her again and she suddenly stood, angry at her own weakness, you knew. She cast the charts onto the table and you looked closely at them. Right away you could see her mistake and how to correct it. A simple matter of degree of latitude.

But how to show her this you wondered, with

no way to write the proper coordinates?

"Look closely Talia," you told her. "Look again at your mistake." At first you did not know if she could still sense you, so still she was. "Please, Talia." You concentrated on the proper latitude, wishing her to look.

Then she did; bending close she again looked at the mark that incorrectly marked their position. Slowly, delicately, you placed your forefinger upon the mark and then moved it, ever so slowly acrossed the page. When you stopped at the correct place you told her softly, yet firmly, "Here, Talia."

To you own amazement and relief, her eyes followed the unseen movement of your finger and stopped when you did. Again the puzzled look but only briefly. Then suddenly she smiled and the room brightened noticeably.

"Of course!" she exclaimed, excited, and yelled, "Boys, I know where we are!" Then she ran from the cabin, charts in hand.

You had returned to the Star People's ship, the captain allowing you all the time you desired to see them safely to the islands.

Being painfully low on supplies they wasted no time and were quickly out to sea again, heading south. You had then told the captain you wished him to take back the helm.

"We will let the ship drift awhile," he said then asked if you would like to be a member of the crew or perhaps a passenger.

"I can think of no destination," you admitted.

He smiled. "You will think of something and when you do I will ask again."

The ship held its position over the Atlantic till night fall. You busied yourself aboard with stowing the silken sails, when suddenly an image of Talia came to you. She was standing alone on the deck watching the stars. You thought you could hear her calling your name.

"I know it was you who was in the cabin, Westly. I just know it," she said. You went to the port side and saw that the ship had drifted to only a short way above your old home, and what you had heard was real. She was there; happy, smiling and you called to her.

"I know you can hear me Westly. I'm looking for you as you asked." She closed her eyes as she continued. "Forever is too long to wait and I know that when you can you will bring the Star People with you."

"Forever is too long to wait," you agreed, then recalled the captain's words. Consider the moment, and you decided that you wished this moment to show Talia you were with her.

At first nothing seemed to be any different but Talia's face showed otherwise. She looked directly up at you and screamed. This brought Nine and Seven to her side and you began to will the ship away so as not to frighten her further, but she raised a hand.

"No, Westly, please do not go."

"Do not be frightened of me ever, Talia," you told her.

"No, never," she said now smiling. The boys watched her closely, clearly worried, but keeping a respectful distance.

Talia said, "You came with the Star People, just as you promised."

"It is a wonderful ship and crew," you told her.

"Are you happy?" she asked.

"When you are happy Talia, I am happy also."

She frowned. "I miss you Westly."

"And I you," you agreed then added, "All you have to do, is think of me Talia, as you do at this moment and I will come to you."

"I wish I could come with you." she said.

You smiled. "Do you wish to leave the ship and the boys now?"

"No," she admitted. "We were going to finish charting the inside islands then Nine wishes to see what lays further south."

"You see, you have much still to do on this voyage," you said.

"What are you going to do?" she asked.

Without hesitation you replied, "I will be very busy as well. I have much to learn if I am to captain such a vessel as this myself one day."

She smiled and said, "Oh Westly, I wish to know every detail. Will you come for me? Will you not forget me?"

"Never will I forget and when you wish I will

come."

By now Nine could no longer hold back and begged Talia to go below and rest.

"Do as he asks, he knows what is right for you," you told her, then said, "Just think of me thinking of you."

She had to force herself not to cry in front of you and only nodded.

"Be happy my love," you told her, and she managed to say, "My love..." before she turned and ran to the deck below. You also began to turn away when you saw the captain approaching, his expression happy.

Leaning over the railing he called down, "Good night, sons."

You also looked over to see Nine and Seven smiling and waving at the ship as it drifted upward into the night.

Talia 1698 Barbados

Talia was without Westly and unsure where she should go. Each way she might choose would leave her equally alone. Westly had suggested going south to uncharted waters, but provisions were low. Seven and Nine would stand with her decision no matter the course, but that only made the choice all the more difficult. Much pain she felt, and anger at herself for not knowing what she should do. Nightly she watched the stars, looking for Westly so that he could tell her how to make a choice; how to live the rest of her life. Three days and nights passed this way and still she was no closer to knowing an answer. But a choice would have to be made upon the forth day, for then the drinking water would be gone.

She stood alone that morning, watching the dawn and scorning it's easily made decision to rise and light the day. Mostly she scorned herself for her jealousy of Westly's escape- no longer would he be forced to decide their fate or make decisions as to the course of their destiny. Talia was set upon her anger of her indecision and said aloud to the bright sun, "Give me none of your light for I know not how to see it." Bowing her head in despair she noticed an even brighter light through her tears. It was the necklace of bees reflecting the dawn. So bright was the gold it threatened to blind her, but she would not look away. She called for the boys who came quickly at her voice. "To the south," she told them, "we go south."

Nine and Seven wondered how they would fare without drinking water, but said nothing. To see again Talia with her mind set was enough, and they steered the ship southward. Many leagues were they able to cross as they cleared the small islands that had hidden them and soon found themselves where no maps could show. The gulf stream behind them to the north, they let the winds carry them south. Talia would have to wait for night to check their position against the stars. But clouds were building. None of them said a word that day, but all were secretly afraid. By nightfall it was overcast, and Talia ordered that they drop anchor. Nine informed her that it was too deep for anchoring where they were.

She could see the fear upon their faces and smiled bravely. "Then we will drift." she told them and they lowered sails. She gave the last of the water to them, telling them there was more when there was none. Nine and Seven took the first watch; though Talia slept little so worried was she that her choice had doomed them. Again she watched the morning alone, but the clouds hid the dawn from her. Even the gold of the necklace seemed dull in the haze.

While Talia stood alone upon the deck, Seven and Nine watched from a small distance away. They knew that the water was gone and the winds spoke of no rain to come. Nine told Seven in a whisper, "We must call them."

Seven shook his head. "But then she will know."

"Yes, but it cannot be helped." Nine insisted, and frowning, Seven agreed. They went to Talia. She was surprised at their serious expressions.

"You should be resting a while longer." she told them smiling, "We will be very busy today."

Seven turned away to hide his frown and Talia asked Nine why he did so. Instead, Nine asked her, "What will we do today with this ship?"

Talia thought what she might say, yet there were no words. Nine nodded. "We know our condition. You have been as a mother to us and have shown your love. Now we will do the same for you."

Even as she tried, she could not hide her tears from them any longer. "I have doomed us," she told them. "Our water is gone and we are lost upon the waves. I have failed you. I have failed Westly and I have failed myself. I should never have left with Westly in the first place." She tried to turn away but Nine held her hands tightly within his own. She found herself amazed at the strength they possessed. Still ever so serious, he asked again what she would do with the ship that day. "Do you not see my dear Nine, I know not what to do?"

"Then give the ship to us." he told her. Startled, she asked what he would do with it. "You cannot ask," he replied. "You must give it to us."

Now Seven faced her. "You must trust us as we

have trusted you."

Talia now pulled her hands free. "This is not possible," she told them kindly. "You are but children. I will think more and find a way to save us."

"What way will you find?" Nine asked. "We have no time left."

She knew he was speaking the truth. She told them, "If you have a plan you must tell me."

But Seven replied, "You must give us the ship."

So tired she was, Talia almost began to chastise them, but their faces, so serious, stopped her. "Very well," she told them. "You have fought bravely for this vessel. As it's Captain I give it to you."

The boy's nodded and Nine said, "We accept."

Seven took her hand and said, "Go below and rest. As Captain's that is our first order."

"But what are you going to do?" she asked.

"You must trust us." Nine told her, then added very serious, "Do not come upon the deck- we will call you when it is time."

She began to ask, "Time for what?" but their expressions stopped her.

Talia went below to the cabin, but she could not rest. She felt she should not have given the ship to them, for since they were to perish she should have been the one to face God as Captain and pay for her failure. She thought she should pray but could think of no words to explain, so instead she spoke to Westly- maybe he would hear her upon that magnificent flying vessel. She told him to forget her, for she had failed, but to save the boys if he could, since they could survive a few more days with the water she had given them. Her thoughts were interrupted by the voices of Seven and Nine. They seemed to be singing in their own language, but so softly that she could not make out any words. She was about to go up but decided against it. Perhaps they were praying to their own gods, she thought, and the thought brought new tears to her eyes.

She had not realized that she had fallen asleep, so when a sudden crash of thunder woke her, she wondered if she was but dreaming. She could hear a fierce rain hitting the ship. Yet when she arose, all was silent. She sighed at her fantasy and called for the boys.

"Come out!" Nine called to her, and when she went upon the deck both were smiling, and Seven held out a cup of water to her.

"It rained?" she asked as they showed her the full barrels of fresh water, and they nodded. Only after she had drunk did she notice the deck and sails were dry.

"How can this be?" she asked.

"We have water," Seven told her. "Is that not enough?"

She began to ask again, but Nine shook his head. "You cannot ask us. We are the Captains of this ship."

Talia knew she would receive no answer by pressing them, so she instead drew them close and said, "You must be angels from the heavens."

They busied themselves with preparing a meal of potatoes and hard bread, and while eating Talia tried to decide what they might do next. There was no way of knowing their position upon the ocean without the fixed stars to guide them, and the sky was yet heavy with clouds. Although they were always careful with the supplies, their food would last but a few days more, and Talia estimated that they were at best five days from land if there was land at all. She watched as the boys did their usual chores, amazed at their smiles, as they actually seemed to enjoy it. They even splashed water upon one another as they washed the morning's dishes, laughing as they called each other "Captain Nine" and "Captain Seven". When they had finished they ran to her and asked for their daily English lesson, usually reserved for this time.

"Perhaps later," she told them. "For the present we must discover where we are and where we should go."

"I know where we are," Seven replied. "We are here."

She smiled, thinking it was a game. "Then where shall we go from here?" she asked playfully, and was startled when he pointed west and said simply, "Over there."

"What is over there?" she asked, and again he said simply,

"Over there."

She turned to Nine and asked if he knew what

his brother was speaking of. "He means over there is not here." he told her then added, here we are lost. Over there we would not be lost.

Talia struggled to remain patient, and said "Do you think there is land over there?"

Nine shrugged, and then said, "Where we think there is land there will be land."

Talia unrolled Westly's chart, which she always kept close, and pointed to their position as much as she could guess at it. The onionskin paper showed land only to the north many days away with the trade winds against them. To each side of their position the chart was empty.

"You see?" she told them. Using her finger, she drew a line from the known land south to their guessed upon position. "We expected the continent to continue south, but it did not," she explained. "Instead we found we found only islands, and now they too are gone. There is no more land to the west. Now perhaps to the east."

Nine shook his head and said, "That land is too far... many years away."

Now Talia sighed, her patience wearing thin. "What is it that makes you think there is land to either east or west?" she asked.

Seven smiled. "There is always land."

Nine punched his brother lightly on the arm and said, chuckling, "She already knows that. She wants to know how we will get to the closer one."

Seven replied with proud dignity, "Because we

are the Captains and we wish it so."

Talia again sighed and said, "But wishing does not make it so."

Sevens smile turned to a puzzled frown, and he looked at Nine who patted his shoulder reassuringly.

Then serious, Nine told Talia, "You are right to say that, but it is true that wishing makes it possible. Wishing is the only way to make it possible. Did you not wish as we did, to be free of chains and ropes and to decide your own destiny?"

"Of course," she told him, "but I did not wish to lose Westly, and I did not wish to be lost upon the seas."

"You have lost nothing," Nine replied. "Are we still captains of this vessel?"

"Would your ship be lost?" Talia asked, "for no crew would follow a captain who is lost, especially with no supplies."

Nine nodded. "We are lost, but the land is not lost. We will not be lost when the land is found."

"We waste our precious time with this game, boys," Talia said, no longer able to hide her frustration.

"Our only reasonable course is back to the north." She stopped their protests by continuing quickly, "Perhaps we will meet another ship who can trade with us for supplies." She turned away from them, but could feel their disappointment. More gruffly than she intended she ordered, "Prepare the sails, we will tack into the wind."

She walked to the helm and when she turned, was startled to see that Seven and Nine had not moved. Never before had they defied her, and she felt herself becoming angry to hide the hurt she felt. "Prepare the sails!" she said again.

They remained motionless for another moment, then suddenly Seven stomped a foot upon the deck, turned, and headed for the rigging. Meanwhile, Nine remained steadfast.

Calming her voice, Talia said to him, "Your brother will need your help."

"Why do we return north?" he asked.

"It is our only hope," she stated. "When we have supplies we can then choose another course."

Nine approached her slowly, his dark eyes so seriously fixed upon hers that she looked away.

"There has never been hope for us in the north," he told her. "There will be no hope for us now to the north. What we have left there will be waiting to greet us again."

Talia had learned to love Seven and Nine as her children, love Westly as her husband; but now as she listened to the older boy speaking so maturely she felt as if she were the child, trying to defend her own immaturity. "Maybe we should return to what we left. Maybe we were fools all along for believing we could have something else. As things are now Nine, we will surely die. If we return, perhaps we will find mercy." She kept her eyes fixed upon the helm, but could not stop from hearing his reply.

"You speak of hope and mercy. Before your words were of only dreams and tomorrows. How can you have changed so much?"

Her anger seemed to swell and roared within her. Not allowing Nine to continue, she yelled, "Because Westly is dead, and his dream is with him upon the flying ship! He sees not us or our misfortune. He was magic to us and he is gone."

"The magic is not his alone," Nine insisted, but Talia shook her head.

"I will hear no more of this. Do as I say and help your brother." The moments seemed an eternity as she waited for him to follow her command, yet he remained steadfast. Already she regretted her outburst, and finally asked him softly, "Will you defy me?"

"No," he said firmly, then added, "but we will not return to the life which we know awaits us to the north." With that he turned quickly and joined his brother.

They did not speak for the rest of the morning, and Talia felt they had made good time and distance. If the wind continued, they might run into the shipping lane within three days. Towards afternoon she set the boys to fishing on the hope of stretching their meager supplies. A few small ones were caught, and these she prepared for their dinner. The boys followed her orders with no complaint, but also clearly without joy. She let them brood, deciding she would explain her plans better to them the next morning. They lowered sails to drift for the night, but with the stars hidden by the clouds, she knew not which direction.

Tired in both mind and body, she gave the first watch to them and went below to rest. At some point she fell asleep and dreamt of the boys as they had been when first she had seen them bruised and beaten. Then the image changed, and she was below deck listening to them as they sang prayers in their own language. Only this time, she could make out a few of the words, which she had learned from them.

"The dreamer cannot awake..."

"The night will not see the day..."

"We know not how to show what we can see to the eyes that remain closed..."

"We know not how to tell what we know to the heart that will not hear..."

Then a voice, strong and manly, replied to them softly, "There will be no light in the power of the quiet ones," and Talia realized it was English. Her surprise at that seemed to awaken her, and she crept up upon the dark deck. The boys were still on the crow's nest, maintaining their watch, but she thought she could see Seven's small arm pointing before the ship.

She peered into the darkness of that direction, and saw a small star glittering glittering brightly between the only visible break in the clouds. Desperately, she looked for any other star to gauge their position by, but there were none. She remained still for a long while, to see if the clouds would continue to part, but they remained motionless; neither widening the small space, nor moving to fill it in.

Guessing at its distance from the horizon, she returned to the cabin to light the lantern and check the charts. As she studied them she suddenly noticed that the ship was moving; she could feel its pull against the ocean. With lantern in hand, she raced to the deck, and holding the light before her, she looked over the side, fearful the ship had been caught in a current. Yet the waves pulled past them as the ship cut through the dark water. There was no current dragging them, and no wind to push them, no force at all to move them.

"Lost forever at sea." The phrase kept running through her mind, and she worked all the more quickly, her fingers searching in the dark for the bolt that secured the anchor's winch. As she finally found it, she was surprised to notice that she was thinking of her old life, before Westly and his magical freedom, before the Master and his cruel slavery, to when she was a child. She had always managed to keep those memories within a safe, comfortable haze, yet now they seemed clearer than the winch before her. She could hear her mother's voice as the woman explained from her deathbed;

"Do not cry for me Talia, for it is to God's grace that I go. Hard we worked in this new land and never did we know what awaited us upon the morrow. I wish I did not have to leave you so young, but leave I must, to make your own way. So I tell you, dearest Talia, worry not of tomorrow; only trust that it will come.'

Her mother had died that night, and the next day her father had given her to the Master of the Harbor, not knowing what else could be done with his young daughter.

Talia was flooded with sudden emotions, wanting to hate her parents, yet not able to blame them for their desperate choices.

"Tomorrow!" she whispered harshly to no one and slammed her fist against the bolt, sending it flying onto the deck. The anchor dropped quickly; she heard the familiar sound as it hit the waves. And while she knew the water would be too deep for it to find a hold, she knew at least the ship would slow from it's drag.

Running to the side of the ship, she listened closely to discover how well her efforts had worked, and was dismayed to realize that the vessel had not slowed at all.

"We must raise the sails!" she called loudly, now racing to the mast.

Nine placed his hand upon hers as she reached for the main rigging line and said, "But there is no wind."

"We have to do something!" she insisted. "We must slow this ship!

Nine began to protest and Talia grabbed him firmly by the shoulders and declared, "This is not a game Nine, we must stop the ship!"

He looked at her a moment, then nodded and said, "I will get Seven."

She released him, relieved to finally receive their cooperation and she busied herself with the rigging's knots. She had untied the first, and had begun the second when she felt the ship reducing speed rapidly. By the time she had reached the side of the deck the vessel had stopped it's motion completely, the oceans waves lapping gently against the hull. Amazed, she looked for the boys and found them nearby, watching her.

"We have stopped." she said, more a question than a statement.

Nine nodded and Seven said simply, "I am sleepy. May I go below now?"

For a moment Talia said nothing, but remained motionless to be certain the ship had truly stopped. Her heart continued to pound from the excitement, and she noticed her hands were trembling, but all else was quiet and still; the ship had stopped. Sighing her relief, she bent to one knee and drew the boys into her arms, hugging them tightly. She felt their small arms encircle her neck and she held them closer.

Though she had wished to hold them this way forever, she did send Seven below to his bunk, while Nine helped her to retie the sail's rigging. Once secured, they searched with lanterns for the anchor winch's holding bolt and after a few minutes feeling upon the deck with their hands, Talia told Nine to follow his brother to sleep; they would leave the anchor to drift and find the bolt by daylight in the morning.

Then, as Nine turned to leave, Talia asked, "Nine, are you certain you saw nothing hit the ship?" When he nodded, she added, "A whale perhaps? Or a serpent?"

"I saw nothing but the star," he stated, and then smiling he suddenly reached for her hand and kissed it. He went below leaving Talia alone; now also smiling as she held the hand the boy had kissed over her heart. She knew he had learned it by watching Westly and it warmed her heart to think how his presence would always live in Nine and Seven. Already mature beyond their years, Westly had instilled in them a fierce determination that, no matter the odds, there was always a chance. With all they had been through, so much in such short years, they had never once cowered from danger or the unknown, like a ship following a lone star under it's own power.

Recalling the star brought Talia from her memories and she went to the very fore of the ship. Just as she reached the railing and looked into the sky, she saw the clouds move in to cover the open space. The star was still there, sparkling, and she looked closely, attempting to identify it before it was hidden by the approaching clouds. The star seemed large, as large as Venus, but it glittered wildly, flashing intense colors of all hues unlike the fair planet's steady white light. She thought perhaps the star only appeared so brilliantly because it was alone in a dark black sky, and therefore could be any number of smaller stars. She went through all the names she could recall; Betelgeuse, Spica, Vega, etc, but none seemed to fit the description and place for that time of the season. Westly had taught her everything she knew about navigation and the sciences of the ocean, and while he had always maintained that she was the perfect student, she now wondered if her own ability was lacking. Maybe there was something she had forgotten or misinterpreted---there was so much of what Westly had told her that she felt she had not understood to begin with. His knowledge seemed as wide as the earth itself, and he had a wisdom that went beyond even that; rooted in the belief that anything was possible, whether he was confidently following a seagull to the school of fish that would soon be their dinner, or judging the speed of the ship by spitting into the ocean, or promising her that he would return to her after his death and bring people from a distant star with him.

It was then Talia realized that the clouds, which moments before were moving to cover the star, were once again motionless. She looked about her, and finding the sky as dark and overcast as before, turned back to the star. It seemed all the more luminous to her now, the brilliant twinkling like flashes of the brightest colors she had ever seen. She thought this must be her imagination for no star would glitter in such a way. She shielded her eyes with her hand so that her vision could adjust to the darkness, then attempted to judge again the star's magnitude. But while her sight was shielded she kept her eyes open and something caught her glance from below. Looking down, she saw light reflecting upon the necklace about her neck. It was faint, but clearly visible as it danced upon the golden bees. Slowly she lowered her hand. Now she was certain; it was indeed larger than any star or planet.

"Is it coming closer?" she asked aloud.

"I am close Talia." came a soft reply. Talia spun around, expecting to face an intruder upon the ship but the deck was empty.

"Do not be afraid my love." She could not tell from where the voice was coming, but she knew to whom it belonged.

"Westly," she called, her original shock turning to joy, "Where are you?"

"I am very near Talia. We will see each other soon, very soon."

Talia pointed to the star. "Are you there Westly, upon the flying ship?"

"I am my dearest."

"Can you not come to us now Westly? We need you."

"We must wait but awhile yet Talia. You have been so brave, more than any man could ask,"

"But I have not been brave Westly. I have lost us upon the ocean, and our supplies are about finished. I do not know how to follow the charts from here,"

"Talia..."

"We have water, but I do not know how we got it,"

"Talia..."

"I have failed as captain..."

"Talia, my love, you have not failed at all. You are the captain of a beautiful ship. The strength of Seven and Nine grows every day within your guiding love."

She could hear his voice so clearly, as thought he stood right before her. She peered closely at the flashing brilliance in the sky, hoping to see the Starpeople's flying vessel but the light was so bright, the colors changing so quickly that her eyes began to sting and she had to look away.

"Soon Talia." Westly insisted softly. "Know, Talia, my promise is not forgotten nor forsaken. We will be together soon."

Talia peered all the more closer at the star, fighting the tear that stung her eyes. She thought she heard Westly chuckle,

"Do not try so hard my love," he said, "We will see one another."

"But when?" She was forced to close her eyes from the light. Westly said, "When indeed?"

Then she saw him within the darkness behind her eyes, just as she remembered, but with a difference, he was wearing a uniform of a captain. He was smiling slyly, like when he had kept a secret.

"Westly, are you a captain of the flying ship?"

He replied, "Just as you are captain of your ocean ship." She felt her heart swell with pride. Westly smiled,

"Just as your ship cuts through the wave of the sea, mine can cut through the waves of thought that separate us. Pilot your ship through these waters and I will pilot my ship through the doubts that separate us. Now I leave you..."

"No." Talia interrupted, opening her eyes without thinking. The image was gone and she feared she had ruined something, but she heard clearly,

"But I will return soon."

Then a sudden wind blew in her face, sending a lock of hair accrossed her eyes, now blocking her view of the sky. In the moment it took her to quickly brush it aside the clouds had moved to fill the space that had opened to reveal the bright star. Once again the sky was dark and completely overcast. She was alone again, but happy now. She waited as patiently as she could for dawn, tempted to wake the boys, but decided to let them rest.

It was Nine who woke in the morning. Going above he was surprised to find Talia mopping the deck, a chore that had been his for so long. Unsure, he returned below to wake his brother. Telling him to be quiet they crept up on the deck. Talia continued happily, humming as she worked. When they could no longer keep their curiosity, they stepped forward and Nine grabbed the handle of the mop and asked,

"Have we slept too long?" Talia smiled. "Not at all."

Seven asked frowning, "What is wrong?"

"What is right you should ask." She could see their puzzlement and laughed. Nine looked at Seven with a look that said 'We have lost her now', but she saw it and said,

"Now dear children, I am not mad. Last night I talked to Westly."

Seven yelled with positively the most excitement either had ever seen. Nine simply hugged her. When Seven settled enough to listen, Talia told them about the conversation and the fact that Westly was now a captain.

To her surprise Nine remarked, "Bout time."

They spent the morning talking about Westly while they finished their chores. When the ship was secure, Talia told them that she now felt they should continue west. Nine held a hand to his brother's mouth to stop another bout of excited shrieking and said, "West it is."

With little wind blowing from the south they were forced to tack and their progress was slow; by dusk there was still no land in sight. Talia found the familiar worries creeping up on her. Without making her thoughts known to the boys she went below and closed her eyes and said softly, "Westly?" To her surprise the reply was immediate; "Tonight."

Startled, she asked loudly, "To the west?"

"Yes."

Talia remained silent, unwilling to risk breaking the connection. Below her feet she could feel the ship flow through the water; it was a soft smooth feeling, cruising freely.

"That is the feeling of freedom." she heard Westly say softly. A moment passed and she ventured, "Westly?"

"I am here Talia, within your heart. Do you see how easily it is done?"

"But I can not see you in my mind."

"It is like the water, to resist will cause waves. Just allow your thoughts to flow of their own accord, I promise they will lead you to me."

"Yes, I do see. But I do not think I can keep the water still. I do not want to lose you again."

"You have never lost me nor shall you ever. When you worry and doubt my love a wave blocks your ability to see and hear me, but that does not mean that we are drifting apart. Remember that Talia, no matter the size of the swell."

Talia listened attentively but she did not like the sound of waves blocking her from him. "I fear the distance."

"If that is a friend of Talia, we have no need of such friends. I must say farewell for a time, I too have preparation. Tonight my love."

She had to fight the urge to shout for him to stay, but she understood. A little sad she opened her eyes and started up the stairs. She could hear the boys playing and just before she reached the top she whispered,

"I love you Westly."

"And I love you, Talia."

She was sure that he had left, and the clear reply surprised and delighted her. Night fell cloudy and very dark. No one felt like sleeping and they stood together watching the western skies. Without the starts to know the direction they could only guess at the direction the ship was headed. Talia tried to keep her mind flowing freely like the water but she found herself nervous, so she asked the boys to sing. Usually when she made this request they would sing to her in their tongue. Tonight however they both began with a song she had sang to them when they first came aboard, a lullaby, 'rock the cradle'. She did not know they knew it and she found herself calmed by it. Their voices were so soft that she felt she might be lulled too by it. Then she realized all at once that she was watching the star glittering before her. She was certain she had not closed her eyes or looked away, but simply found herself just watching it. "Look." she shouted, pointing.

"Westly!" Seven yelled, waving at the star as thought he could see Westly waving back. Nine hugged Talia and she kissed him in return. They were laughing with joy when Seven asked, "Mother, tell us what he is saying."

She looked at him and said, "I can only hear him when he speaks to me in my heart."

Nine told her with a wink, "That is what he

141

means."

Talia was too happy to wonder how they knew about that, and apologized, "I am too flustered right now."

Again Seven asked her to tell him, "But what is he saying?"

Nine punched him lightly and said, "Give her a moment to listen silly."

To her amazement they both fell silent, motionless, watching her. She said hesitantly, "But I do not hear anything."

Giving her a meaningful frown, Seven motioned impatiently by drumming his fingers upon his hips, like she did on occasion. Talia tried to still her mind, but it seemed to race without her. She wanted to concentrate on the star, but Seven and Nine continued to watch her. "I can not," she began, then heard clearly,

"Do not try so hard, flow with your thoughts." She motioned with her finger to her lips to be quiet and saw Seven smile.

"Know that I am here." Westly affirmed and Talia repeated it to the boys. "When morning comes there will be land in sight. Follow it until you see the shore turn to white cliffs." Talia repeated the words then she heard him say, "You boys have become men, now I will expect you to behave as such. I am proud of you both. You and your mother have been very brave, and you will need your bravery still."

Talia finished telling them that when Seven

suddenly said, "Ask him when I will be able to use his sword." Showing her surprise, he added, "Please?"

Talia was taken aback by the requested sword, since he had never mentioned it before and was just as surprised to hear Westly reply, "When I promised." She told Seven and he nodded happily. Talia asked aloud, "Will you land so that we may see you?"

"I will, but not here, my love. Ask again when the cliffs are in sight. Now I must ask something of you."

"Anything." she stated.

"Tonight you must trust me and relinquish control of the ship to the boys. Be most willing Talia or my plan will not succeed."

She said, "I do not understand."

"At the sound of my voice you know that I am near, now will know that I am really here. When Seven wishes he can speak to me at any time, he and Nine will be the chord that lessens the distance between us. Watch, by all means, but do not interfere. Trust that it is my wish."

Still unsure of what he was saying she said, "I trust you."

"That is love in its purest form Talia. Now we begin. My love, be as strong as I know you to be. Now tell Seven to take his watch at the crow's nest."

Talia repeated the words to the boys, and Seven bounded off to his station.

Nine asked, "And me?"

Talia paused to listen. A moment went by and

she thought Westly must have left, and about to tell the boy so, she was stopped when Nine said to seemingly no one,

"Yes, I understand." And then he put his hand in Talia's and held tight. She asked what he had heard and he replied, 'To hold your hand and not to let go."

They watched Seven go upward to the crow's nest, disappearing around the other side of the main mast. Talia returned her gaze to the brilliant star before her, looking for a change in its brightness. She could feel Nine's hand press tighter against her own and it comforted her. She was scared, for reasons she could not define. Around her she suddenly felt a cold wind. She looked toward the mast just as Seven arrived at the crow's nest.

"What will your brother do?" she asked Nine.

"How would I know?" and she realized he was as nervous as well.

Very close to them, but outside of the ship they heard Westly say, "Now Seven."   All eyes turned upon the boy only to see him point at the star with his right hand. A moment passed this way, and Nine sighed and whispered, "Would we wait for the morning?"

Talia whispered back, "We will wait, if we must."

But then Talia noticed a breeze blowing upon her face, and Nine said, "We are moving."

Talia remained very still, to see if she could feel motion. She could, and practically dragging Nine with her ran to the side of the ship. They could hear the bow cutting through the water. Running back to their viewing place they looked again at Seven, still pointing before him at the star. Both stood silent, to watch the star but it seemed to remain still, growing neither brighter nor closer. Talia wanted to shout for Westly or for Seven. It was more difficult than anything she had ever tried, just remaining still. Even in those hard days with the Master she had always been able to do something if only to go to church to escape his wrath.

Westly had told her not to interfere and she now repeated his words over and over again. "Trust me."

But suddenly she noticed the ship had picked up speed and continued to do so. Nine now pulled Talia with him to the very front of the ship, looking overboard. Talia looked too, knowing what he was looking for. but there was no rope pulling them. Seeing nothing they returned to their watch where they took turns watching Seven and the star. Both seemed motionless as thought nothing was happening. Now the ship was moving so quickly that their hair was blown behind them, faster than full sails in trade winds. Talia could feel her heart pounding as well as the rush of water beneath her feet. In her mind she called for Westly. but her mind was too riddled with fear to notice if she heard a reply.

As suddenly as the ship had gained speed it

began to slow, quickly coming to a floating stop. Nine looked at Talia with concern and puzzlement, but she could only shrug. They looked up at the crow's nest, only to see it empty Only then did Nine release Talia's hand, sprinting towards the mast, obviously afraid for his brother. Talia felt her heart stop with fear, when she felt a tug from behind. Spinning around she found Seven yawning and rubbing his brown eyes.

"May I go below now?"

Talia reached for Seven, quickly checking his body for injuries. Finding none she felt his forehead for fever, but he seemed fine, if a little sleepy. By then, Nine had joined them, running to hug his brother with such force he almost knocked him down.

Nine said gruffly, "Where were you?"

Talia said, "Be nice, Nine." She turned again to Seven, bending to one knee to be able to face him, and asked, "Are you all right?"

Seven looked sincerely puzzled. "Of course. What is wrong?"

Nine sighed impatiently, "Why ask us? What happened up there?"

"Nothing." he replied.

Talia stopped Nine from asking again, seeing how obviously tired the younger boy was. She said, "We can talk about this tomorrow. Seven, yes you may go below. Will you be alright alone?"

Seven frowned and remarked, "I am not a baby, you know."

Talia smiled and said truthfully, "No, you

certainly are not."

After he disappeared below, Talia and Nine looked at each other, clearly ready to ask the same question, "What just happened?" but neither asked. A moment passed is silence as they looked at one another, then Talia asked softly, almost afraid to, "Nine have you ever seen such a thing?" she gestured to the front of the ship.

Nine looked thoughtfully in that direction, then at the sky where they had watched the star, then said just as softly, "I think maybe I have, but it is hard to remember." Talia wanted to ask him to explain, but he seemed lost in thought, so she just watched him. Finally he said so softly she barely heard,

"When the men took us from our home, I decided not to remember. Seven did not want to forget," his voice trailed off into silence again and Talia put her arm lightly around his shoulders, to let him know he was no longer alone. Then Nine looked at her, fighting back a tear. "I told Seven not to remind me of those days. That was wrong. Now I can barely remember."

"Tomorrow, when I ask him you need not be there to hear Nine." Talia explained, 'You did nothing wrong, even I have done the same with many memories."

Nine shook his head, "I should not have been so weak, my brother is and always has been stronger than me. But I will not make the mistake again. I wish to know also. "Are we family?"

Talia knew it was not a question but a statement. She nodded, and Nine continuing looked again into the sky,

"Many of my old people believed that one day our race would be destroyed by the force of one ship. Of course no one really believed them. After all what sort of ship was there that could hold a city?"

When he paused, Talia said, "No one could have known the force of the Europeans, Nine."

"Our elders did, and they tried to prepare. They spent all their days hiding our writings deep in the jungles, and making caves in the stone to hold their magic amulets. But mostly they wished to find willing members of my people to teach their spells to." He looked at her seriously, "Usually they only teach magic to their own sons and daughters, but they were so sure of the destruction close by, they were willing to train anyone. My own family..." Again he paused, then said sadly, "Did you know that I made myself forget what they look like?" He did not wait for a reply, "But it do remember the disagreement. I do not know which, but one parent felt their sons should learn and the other did not. We children were very young, but the training was done with magic so it did not matter. So the parents left it up to us. I did not want to be bothered...I was more interested in learning how to trap birds for their feathers," he looked down, squinting as if looking for something, then continued, "I think they were considered very valuable then." He shook his head, "Anyway, I did

148

not care. Seven did." She could hear his voice grow stronger, clearly proud of his brother. "Seven never thought twice but asked to live with a man called..." again he squinted, "Watachet, I think. But a little time was left. Death, where people go to die, I do not remember, not what you call a graveyard," he stopped, unsure of what he meant.

Talia smiled sympathetically, "Do not worry about it."

Nine nodded, "More like another place, like after you are born but not all the way dead? Seven went there with Watachet, and came back knowing all the old man did. We were hunting together as before, for the small monkeys when I got hung up in a vine very high in a tree. If I cut the vine I would fall too far, but I was too caught to climb further. He said from the ground, "Cut it." I thought he was crazy and told him so." He smiled, "He said he would leave me there." He looked at Talia, still smiling, "He was hungry."

Talia remarked, "Sounds like our Seven." He laughed and Talia was glad to see it. "What did you do?" she asked.

He shrugged, "What could I do? I cut it; at least I thought I would get a proper burial, and then I fell. But it took a long time, like all day. I really got bored and yelled for help. Next thing I knew he was standing next to me on the ground and said, "If we missed supper I will not let you sleep any more."" He now returned his gaze to the sky, "I did not know I knew that."

Talia said, "He is very dear to us both Nine. Tomorrow we will ask him about this together."

Nine nodded, "I hope he will tell us."

She thought she heard worry in his voice, "He understands your reasons for not wanting to remember, I am sure."

Nine nodded, but said with doubt, "Hope so…"

There was no time for questions when dawn appeared. To the west land was near. The tide was coming in, threatening to pull them upon the shoals. It was all they could do to get the sails up in time to tack a little further out to sea. Talia took them far enough to still see the white beaches, but far enough to run if another ship was seen. About thirty minutes later they spotted a small stream flowing to the open waters and discussed taking the smaller boat to shore. Talia was as divided as the boys were. Nine felt they should stay aboard until the cliffs were seen, while Seven argued that once the cliffs were seen there would be no place to dock. She knew about the rough waters around the Atlantic facing cliffs, and said finally, "We need supplies very badly. We shall go ashore."

Having made up her mind neither boy protested, but readied the small rowboat. Usually on excursions Nine would stay behind with the ship, and he was surprised when Talia said for him to row. He asked who would watch the ship and she replied,

"Westly will."

Nine asked, "Are you sure?"

Talia now said seriously, "After what we have seen we can trust most assuredly that we are in good hands." When they found anchor, they lowered the small boat and headed to the mouth of the stream, wanting a easy and safe landing. About halfway there, Talia asked Seven softly, "Seven what did you do last night?"

He frowned and said apologetically, "You said I could go to bed. I asked." Talia and Nine had to smile, and Nine clarified, "Before that Seven."

The younger brother thought for a moment, "You mean the star?" He did not wait for a reply, "I pointed at it."

When he did not continue Talia prompted, "No Seven, what did you do to the ship?" Nine added, 'You moved it." Seven shook his head, "I am not that strong." Nine said, loosing patience, 'Then what moved the ship?"

"The star did." Seven said, his features growing angry. He glared at his brother and whispered, "What are you talking about?"

Talia could see what was happening in Seven's mind. He was trying to stop his brother from asking any more about it. Softly she bent closer to him and said, "We do not mean to press you Seven. We just want to know how the ship moved last night. I have never seen such a thing."

Seven reached up and touched her cheek and

smiled, "Is it not enough that we are on land?"

Talia wanted to tell him that she knew about his extraordinary teachings, but thought better of it, so she said instead, "I would like to know Seven. You can tell me."

He looked at her for a moment, as though studying her, then said, "Alright, for you I will answer." He paused long enough to shoot a look of displeasure at Nine, then moved as close to Talia as he could manage in the rowboat. "Westly is in that star. When he told me, I drew him a path in the sky, Westly cast a long rope to me and I held while he pulled us to him."

"There was no rope." Talia pointed out gently.

Seven nodded, "Not the kind you can see." Then he turned to Nine and said stiffly, "I answered the question, are you happy now? I did not move the ship, Westly did."

Talia wanted to ask so much more, but they were approaching the white beach at the left edge of the stream. They pulled the rowboat upon the sand and Talia, usually the one to explore the immediate surroundings alone was happy to tell them to join her. She felt they were protected now. The small stream was about a foot across but it was clear that it usually was much bigger, with boulders littered on each side. Obviously it had flooded there before and they knew they would have to travel far inland to find edible plants and fruits. They stayed close together as they entered the canopy of jungle, moving silently as

Westly had taught them. A few feet at a time they would stop and listen for sounds of movement.

For a while all they heard was the angry birds calling warning at their presence. Then Nine silently drew their attention to shells of nuts piled under a large tree. He pointed up and reached for his long thin throwing arrows. Talia had rarely seen him use them upon the water, light but strong he would shoot them into an empty bag for practice. She watched with fascination as he put the slender arrow into a hollow tube and approached the tree. Aiming above him, he stood motionless for a moment, then suddenly blew a quick breath, barely heard by Seven or Talia. Before Talia could track the path of the arrow, a parrot fell crashing through the branches and landed at Nine's feet. Seven put his hand over his mouth to avoid squealing with pride at Nine's kill, but jumped up and down instead. Talia felt her heart swell with admiration but she kept silent as well. Nine seemed to notice neither of them, but picked up the parrot and twisted its neck to make certain it was dead. He put it in a bag strung at his belt and signaled them to follow. He kept his eyes upward but occasionally looked behind him. Talia was the first to notice smoke in the distance, about a mile ahead. She stopped them and whispered, "We must find what we need here."

They scoured the area for food careful to check for the signs of human life the smoke indicated. Maybe two hours were spent this way and they had little to show for their efforts...a few coconuts, red berries, two more parrots and some squash. When Talia decided they were pressing their luck, she motioned the boys to return to the rowboat. Nine whispered, "What about you?"

She shook her head, "I will be there shortly."

Reluctantly, the boys left with their meager provisions and Talia headed quietly towards the smoke. She moved as slowly and carefully as she could and soon came to a rise where she could see the source. Sitting alone was a very old man, darker than the boys, and with an earring in his ear, a sign of a pirate. She almost bolted away right then but realized that the fire was small, not a guard post. She watched as he poked at a weasel he was cooking and she decided that he had been abandoned there by his fellow shipmates, probably because of his advanced age. She suddenly felt sorry for him, though she knew she could do nothing for him. Relieved that there was no danger she made her way more quickly to the small boat waiting on the beach. Nine ran to meet her and she told them what she had seen.

"Tomorrow we will return for more supplies. For now we have enough."

On the return trip Talia wondered how she might approach Seven with more questions. Going to the aft of the ship, she asked Seven to help her while Nine prepared the birds. When Seven saw that there was nothing to help with, he frowned.

"What do you want me to tell you?" Talia was surprised, "How did you know?"

154

He shrugged, 'The way you look, like you are trying not to hurt me." She hugged him, "I never want to hurt you." He nodded then asked, "What did he tell you?"

As he asked he was clearly angry and Talia asked in reply, "Why are you bothered by what Nine has said?"

"He made his decision, when we left our family. He has lost the right to remember."

She was shocked by his statement. "He told me he was sorry about that."

Seven looked doubtful but said, "Alright, ask me."

"What is wish to know most is how you are in contact with Westly."

He thought for a moment, "The same way as you."

"In your head?" When he nodded then she asked, "When did you begin to hear him?"

"I never stopped." he said flatly.

She momentarily looked away, trying to accept his answer. Without realizing she spoke aloud, she said, "All these years..."

"Yes. You would have thought I was a crazy child if I had told you before."

She nodded and smiled, "Yes, I think I would have. But not now Seven. I will believe anything you tell me."

They were silent for awhile, Talia still thinking of all the years, when Seven asked, "Are there more questions?"

"Why yes." she told him, and was about to ask about his early training when he put up a hand to stop her,

"I must know what Nine has told you already."

Talia told him that she knew about his training with Watachet, that it had been a kind of training that she did not comprehend, then added, "But I would like to."

"It is easy to understand," he said, "you must do two things, believe you can do it and want to do it."

"Do what?" she asked.

He spread his arms wide and said, "Anything."

"But how?" she asked and he sighed and repeated, "By believing and wanting. It is that simple." When Talia frowned he said, 'You said you would believe anything I told you."

She nodded, "I believe you, I just do not understand yet. What else can you do?"   Seven gave a short laugh, "Now I do not understand."

"I mean, what other powers do you have?"

He shrugged, "I have all of my powers, just like you."

"I do not have any powers." she insisted, then added, "At least no powers like you."

He smiled, 'Yes you do. Everyone does."

Talia tried to get Seven to explain his powers further, but he insisted he had told her everything about them. She knew he was being honest and decided that she was not asking the questions properly. She changed the direction of the conversation and asked,

"What of your brother?"

He looked surprised then asked glumly, "What about him?"

"Why are you angry with him?"

He turned away and said softly, "He told our secret." Suddenly he turned to her and said, "He did not have to. Westly did not ask us to. There was no reason to make things more complicated. We kept our secret for a long time, we could have kept it forever."

"But why?" she asked. "Why keep it a secret?"

He cast his eyes downward and shook his head. When it was clear to Talia that he was not going to answer she said, "Remember the day we first met Seven? That horrible man? Why did you not use your powers then?"

Now he looked at her and smiled, "That man now belongs to one worse than himself. I was not big enough to stop him from hurting us, but I knew what was waiting for him. Now I am free and he is not. And do you know why he was beating us? He thought Nine knew where the fountain of youth was. Of course Nine had already forgot."

Talia but a hand on his shoulder and said, "He wishes to change that, Seven. He feels he was wrong to forget his past now."

At first she could not convince him of his brother's sincerity but after a few moments Seven said seriously, "Well, anything is possible." The next day they returned to shore, this time landing the rowboat on the opposite side of the stream.

There was no sign of smoke from the old pirate's camp. They had better luck this trip, finding a wild variety of sweet potatoes and many onions as well as numerous fruits. Nine was determined to shoot enough birds so that they might preserve enough to save, so once they had stored the fruits and vegetables upon the small boat, they followed him further into the jungle. He stayed close to the stream, knowing how the birds favored the coolness of the water. He too was luckier that day, having brought down over two dozen birds in little more than an hour. Then he saw his prize-a bird of paradise-large enough to provide meat for them for two days. He motioned them to wait and crept up to the tall tree alone. Just as he was setting his sights on the bird, something caught his attention from the left. An old dark man was aiming a throwing knife at the same target. Nine knew this was the pirate Talia had seen the day before, but the man was so old and so painfully thin, Nine wondered if he could have ever been a pirate. There was no way anyone could have thrown a knife upward such a great distance and Nine was impressed that he would have even tried. Deciding that the old man must be desperate, he readied himself. Just as the old man threw his knife, Nine released his own arrow. He stayed only long enough for the man to find the fallen bird, then returned to Talia and Seven, telling them only that he did not get the bird.

"Next time," Talia assured him and they returned to the ship with their cargo. They spent the evening cleaning and salting the fowl and just before Talia left them to their watch she told them that if the wind agreed they would sail to the north at dawn.

The morning was agreeable to them in more ways than one, for it was a clear sky that greeted them and a steady breeze blew from the southeast. The brothers were kept busy tacking with the sails and Talia kept a sharp eye ahead at the coastline to their right. It seemed all narrow beach and she began to wonder if Westly might have been mistaken about the cliffs. She tried to get Seven and Nine to rest over the noon meal, but they were so happy to have a direction to follow that they stayed with the sails, contenting themselves with fruit. It was a few hours later when she saw it. They stayed as close to shore as safety allowed and were rounding a stretch of land when suddenly a large building appeared, nestled between the jungle growth and its base below the level of the sea. It was narrow, maybe ten feet wide and tall, thirty feet high perhaps and very long. Talia thought maybe one hundred feet long, stretching length-wise along the ocean. But most startling was its color-though clearly very old and in disuse, it was made of as pure white stone, as white as the beach. Without doubt she knew she had reached the white cliffs.

A small fishing boat came abreast of Talia's ship, and told her of a storm coming, right away. A kindly, ancient man, he helped them to tie down the main sail and steered them to the way to clear the cliffs.

His tiny craft had no trouble using his smaller sail to traverse the point he told them about. It lay just beyond their sight. He offered to take one pass and enter ahead, but none would accept.

Pirates called the point 'Believer" because it was so difficult to round even in good weather, that all prayed whilst doing it. The fisherman left, and Talia and the boys had nothing to do but wait.

The sky was already dark, and the wind was stiff from the south. The ship drifted, but not enough to worry them, and they went below to eat while they could. While making tea, it occurred to Talia that maybe the other's idea of believers point would be the only safe place to survive the storm. She tried to forget such a dangerous suggestion, but it bothered her until she suddenly told Seven and Nine. As she knew, they immediately objected. Then she told them, with the utmost seriousness, that she just knew they would die if they remained where they were.
It was Nine who gave in first, telling her that they could only try. It was slow work, setting the sails again, but as soon as they were free, the ship caught the wind and began the fastest run the old ship had ever experienced. Her crew could do little but hold on and pray. Talia sent her prayers to Westly. yesterday,

and for tomorrows evermore. The infamous point seemed to float by them, and they had to jump into action in order to turn left, into the cliffs. The sea stretched around like a crescent moon, and was just as white. They moved into a mangrove bay and anchored.

They stood motionless for a moment, before the weight of their accomplishment struck them. Many hours passed as the storm raged around them, with the wind stealing their words as they tried to shout to each other. When the storm calmed, and finally spent its fury, they could see its ravishes floating upon the water. There were entire trees and various vegetation as well as many telling planks of wood from other ships.

Yet they were unscathed, and Talia decided it was because of their prayers. She asked Nine to what deity's he and his brother prayed. He told her, at that moment they prayed to her. Surprised, she asked why, and what was their prayer? Seven replied that they prayed to the granter of prayers, and they prayed that she, Talia, had asked for her to pray well. Before deciding their move to intercept Westly, they took the next morning to see what they could of these strange cliff formations. There were places on this side where they could swim to with little beaches to stand on in the low tide. Standing upon one of these beaches for a moment, Talia spotted a glint of gold under a cut in the limestone. It was a bracelet of solid gold, a man's size, with a pin that closed it about the wrist. The only embellishment on it was a tiger, but thinner. Nine suggested a jaguar, though with stripes.

Talia told the boys to stow the sails and find a good place to anchor. As much as she wished to take the rowboat and explore the gleaming ruins, she wanted more to stay aboard the ship and wait for Westly. She tried to remain calm in front of Seven and Nine, and while they waited for nightfall she had them busy preparing the evening meal. She busied herself watching the coastline closely for signs of human life, but the jungle seemed quiet except for the calls of macaws and monkeys. Once, near sunset she thought she had seen a shape move along the edge of the partially submerged building, but it was so small and moved so quickly she decided it must have been an animal.

Finally done with the evening chores and their meal, they settled together on the deck to watch the daylight fade. The sky was clear and they looked at each star as they became bright, for a sign that one was the Star People's ship. About three hours after sunset Nine asked Seven in a whisper, "Do you see Westly's ship yet?"

The younger brother shook his head and replied, "Talia will know."

Nine turned toward her, his eyes questioning but Talia could only shrug and she in turn asked Seven, "How will I know?"

He smiled, still looking at the stars above, "You will know when you know."

She knew he would not be more specific, so she also returned her gaze to the night sky. She thought of how much her life had changed since she was a child, how hopeless she had felt as a shipmasters wife. In those days she could not have conceived of the contentment and love she would feel with Westly, nor the pain and loneliness of losing him. When Seven had told her of his death she felt certain that her own life was over, that she would never again have anything worth living for, but the boys convinced her that their love for her would be reason enough, even if it would never ease her longing for Westly. But then one more miracle in her life would be given her...Westly's promise would be fulfilled and he would return to her, first in spirit and dreams and then, now, she would see him again, perhaps even touch him. Talia sighed and shook her head, thinking suddenly that she might be hoping for too much and she told herself not to expect too much. She had been so lucky so far. Suddenly she was startled when Seven placed his hand in her own.

"You are now disturbing the waves." he whispered seriously.

"What do you mean?" she asked. He pointed at her head, "Go back, do not stop your miracles. Expect everything. Do not disturb the waves."

"But what should I do?"

He shook his head, "It is not what you should do, but what you should not do. Do not disturb the waves. Let them flow. Let your thoughts flow." He pointed again to her head, "Expect everything."

She nodded, though she was still unsure of what he meant. To expect everything... the most she would ever hope to expect was to feel Westly's strong arms about her once again, to feel his breath upon her cheek...

There!" Nine suddenly exclaimed, gesturing toward the long building on the shore, which in the night shone a dark gray. Just above its high roof was a star glittering brightly, more brightly than any other, its colors flashing wildly.

"Is that the ship?" Nine asked Talia, who was about to answer that she was not sure, when Seven whispered to him harshly, "Do not interrupt her thoughts!" then he turned to her and said softly, "Think of him...think of how you wish to see him. Wishing makes it possible."

Talia returned her gaze to the star, and was startled to see that it had dimmed considerably, now only as bright as the surrounding lights. "It's leaving," she began, then felt Seven press her hand tightly.

"Bring it closer." he said.

She took a deep breath and commanded herself to concentrate. Staring at the fading star she imagined it growing brighter, coming closer, bringing the Starpeople's ship with Westly aboard. 'It must come closer,' she thought 'I must see Westly again. He promised and he would never break his promise.'

"No my love, I would never break my promise to you." she heard him say, so near that his voice seemed to come from directly behind her. I love you Talia," he said and this time she felt his breath upon her cheek.

Talia turned around to see Westly standing before her. The first thing she saw was the Captains uniform he wore, radiant white, with gold stitching, and his confident smile. At that moment she found herself paralyzed at the sight, unable to accept she was not dreaming, and when he saw this and put his arm around her slowly, slowly, so she could see that it was real.

"It is I, My Love," he told her. "I am real."

She slowly allowed herself to touch him and when she felt his skin, she fell into his arms and fought not to cry for the joy of it all.

In what seemed only a heartbeat to Talia she recalled moments she had been scared, or doubted her own abilities. She fought so hard to be strong so Westly could keep his promise to return to her. Now she told him, "I believed you."

He replied, "That was all you had to do." She held him tighter and asked if he would leave her again.. The question frightened her, but she felt she had to know. "Never", he told her with a laugh.

She looked at him and he smiled. "How?" she asked.

He replied, "It is complicated to explain here, but we have time on our side now. For the moment, trust that you can come with me now if you wish." She could not wish for any more, she told him, and they kissed as only those who share in time, the love that escapes time.

She held him another moment, longer, and suddenly remembered Seven and Nine. "Did you hear, boys? We get to go with Westly on his ship!"

They were both smiling, careful to watch the reunion from a respectful distance. "No," Nine said, smiling still," we have to stay awhile longer."

Talia began to protest, but Westly's sad smile confirmed her fears. She went to pull away from him, but Westly kept a hold of her hands. "It is not time for that journey, Dearest.

She looked to Seven for support and thought she had found it when he frowned. "I do not think it is fair that we have to steer your ship, Westly."

Westly laughed and told him with mock sternness, "You will have your own vessel in your time."

A while passed, while they shared adventures spent apart. A sudden breeze blew, and Westly looked skyward. "The moment has arrived, Talia. We must be on our way, and leave the boys' way clear."

At first, Talia could not bring herself to say it, but finally she asked, "How can you ask me to leave these boys?"

Seven stated mildly, "We are men, now. You belong by Westly's side, do you not?"

She knew it was true, they were men, and she had learned to know herself by Westly's side. She was not her mothers little girl anymore, or the wife of a tyrant to be looked upon as a possession, nor even a woman alone trying to raise children against the tides of convention.

She had Westly to share life, and that was where she wanted to be.

The end? Or just the beginning?

Authors Bio

Valerie and Bridget were each actively pursuing their soul work when they met in Hawaii thru a mutual friend in 1996. What first seemed a chance encounter would soon prove to be the revelation of a working relationship that spans multiple life-times and hundreds of years. Together they investigated the unending co-occurrences that littered their lives like spiritual signposts. They would discover that those signposts led to a particular destination: a soul-group calling themselves only "Five". And Five had stories to tell.

This story is a reincarnation tale of the authors, presented as a work of fiction.

Read the background story of the two Mayan boys in:

Tales of the Starpeople:
"Child of the Gods"

For more information about Five, go to
www.channelingfive.com
For a free online book and Interactive Spiritual Guidance Aid:
www.theoracle@99k.org

contact us:
wishstar_5 @yahoo.com   bridge579 @yahoo.com